Children
of the
Stones

Children
of the
Stones

Jeremy Burnham
and
Trevor Ray

fantom
publishing

First published in 1977 by Carousel Books
This edition published in hardback in 2013 by Fantom Films
Reissued in paperback 2015
fantomfilms.co.uk

A catalogue record for this book is available from the British Library.

Paperback edition ISBN: 978-1-78196-135-3

Typeset by Phil Reynolds Media Services, Leamington Spa
Printed and bound in the UK by ImprintDigital.com

Cover design by Stuart Manning

CHAPTER ONE

'THIS MUST BE IT.'

The sign post was silhouetted against the afternoon sun, and Matthew shielded his eyes against the glare. His father slowed the battered old Daimler, and peered through the windscreen.

'Can't see a thing.'

'Just have to trust the navigator then, won't you?'

Adam spun the wheel, and turned the car off the main road. Matthew just had time to make out the lettering on the sign. It said 'MILBURY 2.'

His father glanced at him. 'Sure we're on course?'

'Aye aye, skipper.'

'If we waste any petrol, I'll make you pay for it out of your pocket money.'

Matthew grinned. He and his father had always been mates, but the bond between them had grown stronger since his mother died.

And recently, he had made an interesting discovery: that as the son of Professor Adam Brake, he was someone rather special. Mr Corfield, the science master at his old school, was continually using him as a spur to the other boys. 'Come along,' he would say to some unfortunate classmate, 'you don't want Matthew to tell his father you can't solve a simple problem like this, do you?'

Such remarks didn't make life easy. Sometimes the classmate would be waiting in the playground when he came out, and Matthew would have to demonstrate that he could use his fists as well as his slide-rule.

Nevertheless, he enjoyed the awe and respect which his father's name inspired, and when the Headmaster showed him an article in the local paper about the work of 'Professor Brake, Britain's leading astrophysicist,' he felt as if he had scored the winning goal in the Cup Final.

And now he was going to a new school. Only for a term, but a term can seem like an eternity. Would they know who his father was? Would the teacher be as tactless as Mr Corfield? Would there be more fights in the playground? There were so many unanswered questions, so many unknown quantities. Two miles from their destination, he began to feel nervous.

'Dad?'

Adam was intent on the twisting road ahead.

'Mmm?'

'Suppose I don't like this school?'

'Why shouldn't you like it?'

'I won't know anyone.'

'You'll soon make new friends.'

Matthew frowned, disturbed by the prospect of being a new boy again. 'But suppose I don't?' he said. 'Suppose I hate them all? Do we still have to stay for three months?'

Adam glanced at him. 'Yes,' he said firmly. 'If I don't complete my research, the University people are going to want their grant back. And as I've already spent half of it, it might be a bit awkward.'

Matthew nodded gloomily. The fact that his father was brilliant didn't seem to make him rich. He had to supplement his lecturer's salary by writing articles for various scientific magazines, and even then they always seemed to be short of money. If only he'd been an inventor – if he'd stumbled on a brand-new formula for rocket-propulsion or something – then they'd probably be travelling to Milbury in a chauffeur-driven Rolls-Royce. But astrophysicists, no matter how clever they were, didn't seem to be worth much in hard cash.

Matthew leaned forward, took the guidebook out of the glove compartment, and leafed through it till he came to Milbury. There were the two pictures that had so intrigued him when he first started to read about the village: one a photograph of the Stone Circle as it was today, and the other an artist's impression of how it must have looked in 3000 B.C. There were a hundred stones originally – huge black sentinels that surrounded the village in a giant ring – of which fifty-three now remained.

'3000 B.C.!' he said softly, staring down at the guidebook. 'Were the stones really standing then?'

'Some of them. The circle was certainly under construction.'

'So it's older than Stonehenge?'

Adam smiled. 'Considerably older. By the time Stonehenge was completed, the Milbury Stones would have been standing for at least a thousand years.'

'Wow. That's pretty fantasmagorical.'

'Pretty *what*?'

'Fantasmagorical. It means more fantastic than fantastic.'

'It doesn't. It's spelled with a "PH," and it comes from "phantasmagoria," meaning a series of illusions or phantoms.'

Matthew grinned. 'Yes, Professor.'

He used his father's title whenever he began to sound like a lecturer. Sometimes he forgot that he wasn't talking to one of his students, and Matthew resented it. He was eager to learn from such a great man, but as his son, not just another pupil. Teachers were two a penny, but fathers were hard to replace.

Adam frowned at him in mock disapproval. 'Cheeky.' But Matthew knew that the message was received and understood.

Satisfied that they had re-established their special relationship, he turned to stare out of the window at the rolling countryside. The sun was now hidden by clouds, and the dark fields looked suddenly cold and uninviting. It felt more like winter than early summer.

The Daimler growled over the brow of a hill, and Matthew caught his breath. Below them, about a mile away, lay Milbury, looking exactly like the photo in the guidebook. About half the stones were still standing, but the positions of those that had disappeared were marked by concrete pillars, so that at first sight the ring seemed intact. The village nestled in the centre, like an animal asleep in its lair.

The empty road stretched gently down toward it, as straight as an arrow. On either side stood more stones, about fifty metres apart, as if guarding the entrance to a citadel. This must be the famous 'Avenue.'

The car plunged down the hill, and Matthew watched the stones fly past the window. Then he turned to look at the village again, and his heart seemed to miss a beat.

The road ahead was no longer empty. A large grey stone stood in the middle of it, barring their way, at the point where it passed through the edge of the circle. They were racing toward the obstacle at such a speed that an accident seemed inevitable.

'Dad! Stop!'

Adam had apparently seen the stone at the same moment, and stamped hard on the brake. The car skidded to a halt a few feet away from the… stone?

Matthew peered through the dirty windscreen. No, it wasn't a stone. It was a woman in a grey dress. He had been watching so many stones out of the side window that his eyes must have superimposed the image on whoever it was in front of them.

His father seemed just as puzzled. 'Extraordinary. Just for a moment, I thought…'

'I know,' said Matthew softly. 'So did I.'

The woman was plump and elderly. She remained where she was, as motionless as the stones on either side of her. Adam honked the horn impatiently, but she took no notice.

'What on earth does she think she's doing? She can't be blind *and* deaf.' He leaned out of the window.

'Will you please get off the road?' he shouted.

The sound of his voice seemed to startle the woman into life. She bustled toward them, eyes twinkling and rosy cheeks shining.

'Professor Brake?' she asked, bending down and staring into the car.

Adam looked surprised. 'Yes. But how did you…'

'Happy Day to you. I'm Mrs Crabtree.'

'Ah. The housekeeper?'

'That's right. Mr Hendrick asked me to meet you and show you the way to the cottage.'

'Very kind of him. And you. Jump in.'

Adam opened the back door for her, and she eased herself, not without difficulty, into the back seat. ' 'Fraid I'm not getting any younger,' she said cheerfully, settling back on the cushions.

'This is my son Matthew,' said Adam, as they accelerated off down the road.

Mrs Crabtree smiled. 'Happy Day, Matthew.'

'Hello.'

Matthew didn't know what to make of their passenger. She seemed pleasant enough, but her eyes twinkled too much for his liking, and her smile worried him. There was something not quite right about it, just as there was something not quite right about the way she had greeted them. He had never heard anyone say 'Happy Day' before. Perhaps it was a local expression.

His father had told him they would have a housekeeper to look after them during their three months' stay, and he had pictured her just like Mrs Crabtree, a stout countrywoman with apple cheeks and grey hair; but what he hadn't expected was that he should dislike her so much. He didn't know why, but she made him feel uncomfortable. He got the impression she was putting on an act for their benefit.

Matthew had also pictured the place they were renting, 'Hawthorn Cottage,' and this time the reality didn't disappoint him. It was almost exactly as he had imagined: a wicker gate, lattice windows, and a wooden door surrounded by sweet-smelling white flowers. As they climbed out of the car into the warm, still air, his spirits rose.

Adam clapped a hand on his shoulder. 'Not bad, eh?' He turned to Mrs Crabtree. 'Perhaps you could rustle up some tea while we bring in the luggage?'

'Of course, sir.' She winked at Matthew. 'I hope the young gentleman's fond of chocolate cake?'

Matthew felt hostility welling up inside him like indigestion, and he had to swallow hard to keep it down.

'Yes,' he said politely. 'Thank you.'

Mrs Crabtree hurried down the path and disappeared inside the cottage. Adam began to take out their suitcases.

'Looks like we've got a real treasure there.'

Matthew said nothing, and Adam glanced at him in surprise.

'You don't like her?'

'No.'

'Why not?'

'I don't know.'

'You don't usually make your mind up about people so quickly.'

Matthew shrugged, unable to put his thoughts into words. Adam stared at him, frowning. They so rarely disagreed about anything that they had come to trust each other's judgments.

'I expect you'll change your mind when you get to know her better.'

'Yeah.' Matthew picked up two of the cases and carried them into the cottage.

The interior was as bright and friendly as the exterior. The narrow hallway had a low, oak-beamed ceiling and spotless white walls. A ramshackle staircase led up to the first floor. A door on the left led into a comfortable living room, where Mrs Crabtree was laying the table for tea.

Matthew put down the cases, wandered into the room, and looked around with approval. There were vases of freshly cut flowers all over the place, and the crisp, lemon-yellow chair-covers smelled of lavender. This was more than a rented cottage: it was a home.

Mrs Crabtree nodded to three large crates piled up in a corner. 'Those arrived yesterday, addressed to your father,' she said. 'I didn't know where he wanted them, so I told the men to leave them there for the time being.'

'Splendid,' said Adam, appearing in the doorway. He strode over to the crates. 'One, two, three. Yes, all present and correct.'

'The labels say "Handle with care." ' Mrs Crabtree paused on her way back to the kitchen. 'China would it be? Or glass?'

Adam smiled. 'No, Mrs C. Not china or glass.'

'Oh.' She waited expectantly for him to go on, but no more information was forthcoming. A low whistle came from the kitchen, rising to a high screech. 'The kettle,' she said, and rushed out.

Adam turned to Matthew. 'Give me a hand, will you, Matt?' he said, indicating the top crate. Together, they lifted it and set it down carefully in front of the fire.

'Got your penknife?'

Matthew delved into his trouser pocket, and produced the knife which his father had given him for his last birthday.

'Thanks.' Adam opened the large blade and began to pry off the lid. 'Your picture's still in the car. You'd better bring it in before anyone sees it. We might get thrown out of the village.'

'Right.' Matthew turned and ran out of the cottage.

The boot of the Daimler was still open, and Adam had left the picture propped up inside it. Matthew caught his breath, just as he'd done when he first saw it in the shop window. It gave him a weird sensation in the pit of his stomach – as if he was hurtling downwards in a very fast elevator.

The artist seemed to have had a vision, a terrible nightmare which he had apparently painted in his sleep. In the centre of the picture, a ring of people were trying to shield their eyes from a brilliant, blinding light. Some of them had already broken from the ring, and were running away in terror. Those furthest from the light were glancing back, and the lower halves of their bodies had turned to stone. Further away still were complete pillars of stone, and the suggestion was that these massive shapes had once been people. In the bottom right-hand corner, a man was dragging a boy away from the scene. Both had grim, fearful expressions on their faces, as if they were determined not to look back.

All this was eerie enough, but the thing that had first caught Matthew's attention was the fact that the village in the picture was exactly like Milbury – or rather, the drawing of the prehistoric Milbury that he had seen in the guidebook. Adam, too, had been fascinated by the resemblance, and had gone halves with him so that he could buy the painting. They had talked for hours about what it might mean, but neither of them had so far been able to make sense of it. All Matthew knew was that it meant *something*: no one could paint a scene like that by chance.

He was staring at the curious Latin inscription at the bottom, when he heard a footstep on the gravel behind him. He turned, to find a solemn-looking girl peering over his shoulder. She was hugging a school satchel, her thick, raven hair stirring gently in the breeze.

'That yours?' she asked, nodding at the picture.

'Yes,' said Matthew.

'Pretty creepy. It's Milbury, isn't it?'

'I think so.'

'Milbury a long time ago.' The girl looked thoughtful. 'Any idea when?'

Matthew was glad of the chance to display his knowledge. 'My father thinks it's meant to be the Megalithic period,' he said airily. 'The Neolithic or early bronze age in northwest

8

Europe lasted approximately 3000 to 1800 B.C., and in Britain the earliest traces of…'

'All right. There's no need to show off.'

Matthew, realizing he'd sounded just like Adam in one of his 'lecturing' moods, grinned. The girl smiled back, her solemn expression suddenly evaporating.

'Is your dad an expert?' she asked.

'Yes.'

'On painting?'

'No. He's a scientist.'

'Oh.' She glanced at the cottage. 'Just arrived, haven't you?'

'That's right.'

'I heard you were coming.'

'You mean, my father?'

'Both of you.' She suddenly looked serious again. 'It's quite an event when new people come to a village. Specially this village.'

She made it sound as if there was something wrong with the place, and Matthew was curious. 'Why? Don't people come here?'

'Not many.' She regarded him gravely for a moment. 'And those that do have to stick together.'

She turned abruptly and ran off down the road, swinging her satchel. Matthew stared after her, the strange warning echoing in his ears like a distant alarm bell. But what had she been trying to warn him against? Wild animals? Highwaymen? A gang of kidnappers?

His heart beating considerably faster, he picked up his picture and carried it carefully into the cottage. Back in the living room, Adam had opened the crates, and was gently lifting his precious electronic gadgets out of their beds of straw. Mrs Crabtree, holding a teapot she had just brought in from the kitchen, was watching with eyes full of wonder.

'Excuse my asking, sir,' she said, pointing to one of the light aluminum boxes, 'but what's that?'

'It's a magnetometer,' said Adam.

'A what?'

'An instrument for measuring magnetic fields. Do you know what a magnetic field is?'

'No.'

Adam glanced at Matthew. 'Tell her, Matt.'

Matthew set down his picture with its face against the wall. 'It's the field of force that surrounds a magnet,' he said.

Mrs Crabtree looked bewildered. 'Well, we've no magnets here.'

'Ah, but you have,' said Adam. 'You have fifty-three, to be precise.'

'Fifty-three?'

'The stones, Mrs Crabtree. Each one contains a great deal of magnetism, even after five thousand years.'

'Well, I never. And how do you happen to know a thing like that?'

'It's my job.'

Mrs Crabtree looked doubtfully at the magnetometer. 'So that's why you've come, is it sir? To measure the stones?'

'Among other things.'

'Well, I never. You want to be careful, then.'

Adam frowned. 'Why?'

'Sounds dangerous to me.'

'Dangerous? No, no, it's not at all dangerous. Magnetism's a perfectly harmless branch of physics.'

He turned to Matthew. 'Show her your picture, Matt. See if she recognises it.'

Matthew picked up the painting, turned it around, and held it up for her inspection. The effect was astonishing. The colour seemed to drain from Mrs Crabtree's face, her eyes closed, and she collapsed to the floor. The teapot smashed into a thousand pieces.

Matthew looked helplessly at his father. He felt guilty, as if he had frightened a child by telling it ghost stories. Adam motioned him to put the picture away, crossed over to Mrs Crabtree, and lifted her up into a chair.

'Are you all right, Mrs C?'

She didn't answer. Her eyes remained closed, and she was moaning softly to herself. Adam bent down and gently tapped her cheek.

'Mrs C. Wake up.'

Matthew returned and knelt anxiously by her chair. 'What's wrong with her, dad?'

'Fainted. She'll be all right in a minute.'

'Was it the picture?'

'Must have been.'

'That's funny. I mean, I know it's pretty horrific, but I never expected it would make people faint.'

'Neither did I. But the artist would probably have been delighted. I imagine it was just the effect he was aiming for.'

'Hello,' said a deep voice behind them. 'Smashing the crockery already? Hardly an auspicious start to your tenancy, Professor.'

They turned, to see a big, distinguished-looking man standing in the doorway. He had a ruddy complexion, and jet-black eyes which were regarding them with amusement. Matthew guessed he must have been about fifty.

Adam stood up. 'I'm sorry. You have the advantage of me.'

'Then allow me to introduce myself,' said the stranger. 'The name...' He paused, and the black eyes flicked to Matthew. 'The name is Hendrick.'

CHAPTER TWO

SO THIS WAS THEIR new landlord. Matthew had watched his father make out a check to 'R. Hendrick Esq.' for £240 – three months' rent in advance – and he had pictured some doddering old colonel, trying to make ends meet by letting his cottages for the summer. But this man didn't dodder: he stood as straight as a ramrod.

The stranger seemed pleasant enough, but the dark eyes were without warmth. They darted quickly from side to side, taking everything in, yet giving nothing away. It was impossible to tell what he was thinking.

He didn't appear to be annoyed that the teapot had been smashed to pieces, and that a dark stain was spreading over the carpet. He put his hand gently on Mrs Crabtree's shoulder.

'Mary?'

Her eyes snapped open, and she stared up at him blankly. Hendrick's voice took on a sharper edge.

'Mary. Another pot of tea, if you please.'

'Yes, sir. Happy Day, sir.' Snapping out of her trance, she stood up and bustled back into the kitchen.

Adam started picking up the broken pieces of china. 'I'll pay for the damage. We gave her a bit of a shock, poor woman.'

Hendrick looked surprised. 'Shock?'

'Well, it *is* rather macabre.' Adam threw the fragments into the wastepaper basket, crossed over to the picture, and held it up.

For a long moment, Hendrick remained absolutely still. Then he walked slowly over to the painting and peered closely at it, examining every detail.

'Where did you get this?'

'My son found it.'

'Where?'

'In a junk shop.'

Hendrick turned and looked thoughtfully at Matthew. Matthew shifted uncomfortably from one leg to the other, feeling the black eyes boring into him. They were like radar scanners, trying to probe an unidentified object.

Then, unexpectedly, Hendrick smiled. 'Your name, young man?'

'Matthew.'

'*You* bought this picture?'

'Yes.'

'Why?'

Matthew swallowed nervously.

'It looked just like the photographs. Of the village, I mean.'

'Strange. That you should happen to see it.'

The voice was soft, but the statement sounded like an accusation. Matthew felt a further explanation was necessary.

'It was in the window of this little shop. I couldn't see half of it, because it was hidden by an old candlestick. But it was only 50p, so I went inside and asked if I could look at it.'

'Did the shopkeeper tell you where *he* got it?'

'He said he got most of his stuff from country houses, but he couldn't remember which one it came from.'

Adam had turned the picture around and was studying it with interest. 'The resemblance to Milbury is certainly remarkable,' he said. 'The circle must have looked very like this when it was first erected.'

Hendrick moved to stand by his side. 'The people appear to be running away from that bright light in the centre.'

'Like a primitive tribe running away from an eclipse.'

'Yes. An ancient pagan ceremony perhaps. They could have conjured up some sort of apparition, and then found they'd bitten off more than they could chew.'

Adam smiled. ' "From ghoulies and ghosties and long leggity beasties, and things that go bump in the night, good Lord deliver us." '

Hendrick stared at him. 'What on earth's that?'

'It's an old Cornish litany. When I was a boy, my mother hung it on the wall above my bed. I used to think it was very sinister. As a matter of fact, I still do.'

Hendrick bent down to examine the picture again. 'There's an inscription at the bottom,' he said. 'I can't see without my glasses. What does it say?'

'I've learned it by heart,' said Matthew. 'It's in Latin, and it says "*Quod non est simulo dissimuloque quod est.*" '

Hendrick look impressed. 'Can you translate it?'

'Dad told me what it means. It's something like "I deny the existence of that which exists." '

'Really? A rather futile statement, don't you think?'

Matthew had already come to the same conclusion. 'Pretty stupid,' he agreed.

Mrs Crabtree appeared with a fresh pot of tea. She looked very shamefaced, and glanced apologetically at Hendrick, as if begging his forgiveness for her lack of self-control. But Hendrick didn't seem to notice.

'Ah,' he said, rubbing his hands, 'tea at last. You don't mind if I join you?'

Adam indicated a chair. 'Please,' he said. 'Everything we have is yours.'

They sat down and the two men chatted on while Matthew attacked the food with gusto. He had to admit that Mrs Crabtree was an excellent cook. The chocolate cake was delicious.

Hendrick sipped his tea, regarding Adam's electronic equipment with a professional eye.

'Oscillator, oscilloscope, magnetometer. Expensive toys.'

'They're not mine,' Adam told him. 'They're borrowed from the University.'

'You'll be going back, then? When your three months are up?'

'Oh yes.'

'Ever thought of settling down in a place like this?'

'I've thought of it. But I can't afford to retire yet awhile. I've a growing boy to feed, and you can see how much he eats.'

Matthew, his cheeks bulging with cake, felt embarrassed. He knew his father was joking, but did Hendrick know it? Their visitor didn't seem to be the sort of man who appreciated jokes. He swallowed quickly, choked, and felt even more embarrassed when a fit of coughing made him turn away from the table.

Hendrick made no comment. He turned back to Adam. 'Forgive my curiosity,' he said, 'but your wife...?'

'She died,' said Adam. 'Two years ago.'

'I'm sorry.'

'I have Matthew. Despite his voracious appetite, he's a great consolation.'

Matthew began to feel better. To be described as a consolation, even a greedy one, was confirmation that his father needed him. He didn't care what Hendrick thought of him now. Defiantly, he helped himself to another piece of cake.

Hendrick watched him impassively. 'And a future astrophysicist?'

Adam shrugged. 'Possibly. He seems to have inherited a great deal of my...' He hesitated.

Hendrick smiled. 'Talent?'

'Enthusiasm.'

'You're too modest. I read your paper on the residual magnetism of megalithic stone. A very impressive piece of work.'

Adam looked surprised. 'You'd heard of me, then? Before I answered your advertisement?'

'Heard of you? Of course I'd heard of you. Anyone with the faintest interest in astrophysics has heard of Adam Brake.'

Adam poured himself another cup of tea. 'And you have more than a faint interest?'

'I dabble, you know. Inside this Circle, it's difficult not to speculate.'

'I can imagine.' Adam turned to Matthew. 'Finished?'

'Yes.'

'Then why don't you go out and explore? Get your bearings?'

Matthew hesitated. He didn't particularly want to go exploring without his father: it had seemed a perfectly ordinary village apart from the stones, and to understand their significance he needed Adam's expert knowledge.

Hendrick misinterpreted his reluctance. 'The locals don't bite, you know. Everyone's very friendly here. I'm sure you'll find someone to show you around.'

He spoke with such confidence that Matthew suddenly felt certain this wasn't a guess. It was almost as if the big man knew who that someone would be.

But whether he knew it or not, he was right. A well-built boy of about Matthew's age was waiting by the garden gate, munching an apple. His bicycle was propped up against the fence.

Matthew walked slowly down the path toward him.

'Hello,' he said.

'Happy Day,' said the boy cheerfully.

Again the strange greeting. Matthew couldn't understand why it made him so uncomfortable: after all, it was perfectly natural to wish someone happiness.

He opened the gate. 'I'm Matthew.'

'Bob,' said the boy. He held out his apple. 'Like a bite?'

'No thanks. I've just had tea.'

'Right. Off we go, then.'

'I haven't got a bike.'

Bob pointed to a shed next to the cottage. 'There's one in there.'

Matthew opened the shed door, and found a shiny new bike propped up against one of the walls. He wheeled it down the garden path and climbed on. It was just his size.

Bob watched him expressionlessly. 'Okay?'

'Fine.'

'Good.'

He climbed onto his own bike, and cycled off down the road. Matthew had to pedal hard to catch up with him.

'Where are we going?' he asked.

'I dunno. Fancy an ice cream?'

'I haven't any money.'

'I have. We'll stop at the Post Office.'

They turned left down a narrow passage between two houses. Some distance ahead was the girl Matthew had spoken to outside the cottage. She was wandering along, swinging her satchel, and didn't appear to hear them until Bob rang his bell. Then she jumped to one side like a startled rabbit, flattening herself against the wall as they cycled past.

Matthew noticed that she completely ignored Bob. He himself seemed to be the object of her attention, and when he glanced back she was still gazing solemnly after him. He remembered her parting words. 'We have to stick together,' she had told him – an odd, disturbing thing to say.

'Who's that?' he asked Bob, when they had turned another corner.

'Name's Sandra. Her mum looks after the Museum.'

'She stares a lot.'

'Yes.'

'Something the matter with her?'

'Not that I know of. She'll feel better when she's a Happy One.'

'What's a Happy One?'

'Someone who's happy, of course.'

Matthew began to feel annoyed. Everyone in the village seemed to talk in riddles, as if they shared a secret from which he was excluded. Well, he wasn't going to give them the satisfaction of letting them see how frustrated he was. He would play it cool until they decided to accept him.

They reached the Post Office and dismounted, leaning their bicycles against the wall. Bob went in, and Matthew was about to follow when he happened to glance up at a small hill just outside the Stone Circle.

A man was standing motionless on the hilltop, silhouetted against the evening sky. As Matthew watched, he raised a long, thin object to his head, and pointed it straight at the Post Office. There was a glint of silver as the object caught the sun's rays, and it was suddenly possible to see it more clearly. It was a telescope.

It was bad enough to be stared at by the girl, but to be scrutinised by a man with a telescope was too much. Matthew hurried inside, feeling more and more bad-tempered: if only people around here would mind their own business!

The Post Office was more of a village shop. True, there was a small counter at the back with a sign saying 'STAMPS AND POSTAL ORDERS,' but most of the space was taken up with boxes of fruit and vegetables, and the shelves were packed with tins of food. There was a freezer in a corner, from which Bob was helping himself to two ice cream lollies.

The post mistress stood by his side, beaming at him. She was a small bird-like creature with enormous eyes that were magnified by a pair of thick, rimless spectacles.

'That'll be 12p, Bob,' she was saying. 'Sure you can afford it? You don't get your pocket money till tomorrow.'

Bob handed her the money. 'Still got some left from my birthday, Mrs Warner.'

'Good boy. It pays to be thrifty, doesn't it?' She turned and moved toward the till, then stopped as she saw Matthew. The huge eyes blinked at him through the glasses.

'This must be the new friend you were telling me about.'

'Yes.' Bob handed Matthew one of the lollies, and they both started to unwrap them.

MrsWarner opened the till. 'It's nice to make new friends,' she said. 'Old friends are all very well, but it's nice to make new ones. It broadens one's horizon.'

'Yes,' said Bob. 'I'm just showing him around.'

'Well, Happy Day, boys. Enjoy yourselves.'

Matthew followed Bob outside. As he shut the door, he could see Mrs Warner beaming at him from behind the counter.

They retrieved their bikes and wheeled them into the road, sucking their lollies.

'Why do you all say that?' asked Matthew.

'What?'

'Happy Day.'

Bob shrugged. 'We just like people to be happy. Anything wrong with that?' He ran several paces, threw himself over the crossbar, and cycled off down the street.

Matthew was about to follow, when he suddenly remembered the watcher on the hilltop. He turned and squinted up toward the setting sun.

The man was still there, still holding the telescope to his eye. Not for the first time since he came to the village, Matthew felt vaguely uneasy. He threw his lolly stick into a litter bin, climbed onto his bike, and pedalled away as fast as he could.

He turned a corner, and saw that Bob was far ahead, racing toward the crossroads at the centre of the village. Matthew called to him, but he took no notice, standing up on the pedals to get more speed.

In the distance, from the direction of the Avenue, came the sound of an approaching lorry, thundering toward the crossroads. Matthew slowed down, expecting Bob to do the same, but his companion didn't seem to be aware of the danger.

Matthew shouted a warning, but it went unheeded: Bob was pedalling furiously toward the main road. And now the lorry came into view, roaring down the Avenue like a huge black animal. Surely Bob could hear it now? The noise was deafening.

But still he hurtled on. And Matthew realised with horror that if neither of them slowed down, the bike and the lorry would reach the crossroads at exactly the same time. They were on a certain collision course. He stopped and cried out in alarm, but the roar of the lorry's engine was now too great: he couldn't even hear his own voice.

He covered his eyes, unable to watch the inevitable accident. He heard the crashing of airbrakes, the baying of a car horn – then silence. All sound suddenly stopped, as if a television control had been switched off.

Slowly, he forced himself to open his eyes, expecting to see the wreck of a bike, and the mangled body of its owner. But there was Bob, cycling around and around in the middle of the road as if nothing had happened.

'Come on,' he called impatiently. 'What've you stopped for?'

'The lorry. What happened to the lorry?'

'What lorry?'

'You must have seen it. It was coming straight at you.'

'If something was coming straight at me, I'd've got out of the way, wouldn't I?'

There was no answer to that. Matthew remounted his bike and cycled slowly up to the main road. He could see a couple of miles in both directions, and it was completely empty, its surface shimmering in the heat. Could he have imagined the lorry? No, of course not. The crashing of its brakes still echoed in his ears. Then how could it have disappeared? And why was Bob pretending that he hadn't heard it? It was all extremely puzzling…

Adam, meanwhile, was strolling across the village green with Hendrick. They were making for the pub, where

Hendrick had offered to introduce his new tenant to some of the locals. Adam had eagerly accepted the offer: it was a long time since he had had a drink in a real old country pub, and the contacts he made there might prove very useful.

Hendrick hesitated by the door. 'You know, it really is an extraordinary coincidence,' he said thoughtfully.

'What?'

'Your son coming across that picture.'

'Yes. Bit of luck, wasn't it?'

Hendrick frowned. 'Luck?'

'That he got it so cheap.'

'Oh. Yes, I suppose it was.'

He pushed open the door and led the way into the pub. There was only one bar – a long, oak-beamed room with several alcoves leading off it. Adam noted with distaste that there was a jukebox in a corner, but the place was bright and cheerful, and it had its compensations.

Not least among these was an attractive woman who sat alone in one of the alcoves. She had red hair, and wore a smart green trouser-suit which looked as if it had been specially designed for her. She sat perfectly still, playing with the half-empty glass on the table in front of her, and taking no notice of the group of men who were chatting by the bar.

Adam guessed she was in her early thirties. He hadn't looked at another woman since his wife had died, but this one interested him. Her beautifully sculptured face might have been carved out of marble, and he wondered what she was thinking. She hadn't taken her eyes off her glass since they came in.

There was no sign of a male companion, but Adam took it for granted that she was married. Surely she must have been snapped up by now? He glanced at the third finger of her left hand: yes, there was an expensive-looking emerald ring on it. Just his luck!

Hendrick grabbed him by the elbow and propelled him to the bar. The landlord, a big, bald man with huge forearms, moved to serve them.

'Evening, Mr Hendrick. The usual?'

'Yes please, George. And I've brought you a new customer.'

The landlord gave Adam a friendly smile. 'Oh?'

'This is Mr Brake. He's renting my cottage for three months.'

The landlord wiped his hand with a cloth and held it out. 'Happy Day to you, sir. A hard-drinking man, I hope?'

'I like whisky, if that's what you mean,' said Adam, shaking hands.

'Large or small?'

'Large,' said Hendrick. 'It's my round.'

While the landlord was fetching the drinks, Adam glanced back at the solitary woman. 'Who's that?' he asked.

Hendrick turned and contemplated her approvingly. 'Attractive, isn't she? Name's Margaret Smythe. Another new arrival.'

'A summer visitor?'

'No, she's come to work here. She's the Curator of the Museum.'

'Married?'

'A widow. She has a daughter at the school.'

Adam's spirits rose. 'Is she as lonely as she looks?'

Hendrick looked amused. 'There's only one way to find out. Follow me.'

They crossed over to the woman's table. Hendrick put a hand on her shoulder. 'Margaret?'

She looked around, startled. 'Yes?'

'This is Adam Brake. Poor chap doesn't know anyone in the village. Wants to be taken under your wing.'

The woman surveyed Adam with cool green eyes. 'Why mine?'

Hendrick smiled. 'I think he likes the look of the feathers.' He moved back to the bar, leaving them alone. Adam suddenly felt like an awkward schoolboy.

He indicated the bench opposite her. 'May I?'

'Of course.'

He sat down, but was embarrassed to discover that he couldn't think of anything to say. The green eyes were appraising him, and he wondered if they liked what they saw.

'It is true, you know,' he said finally, trying to get some sort of conversation started.

'What's true?'

'That I want to be taken under your wing. I'm going to need your help.'

She frowned. 'What sort of help?'

'I'm a scientist. Here to do some research on the stones.'

'I know.'

Adam stared at her. 'I seem to have had a lot of advance publicity.'

'A village is a small place, Mr Brake.'

'Adam.'

She nodded, as if she had at last decided to accept him. The invisible barrier between them suddenly seemed to disappear.

'I've read everything I can about the Circle,' he went on, 'but nothing to explain why Neolithic Man chose to construct it at Milbury. Perhaps you have some theories?'

She looked down at her glass. 'Oh yes,' she said softly. 'I've plenty of theories.'

'I'd like to hear them.'

'Come to the Museum tomorrow morning. We can talk there.'

'Right.'

'As a matter of fact, there's one mystery that perhaps *you* could explain to *me.*'

'What's that?'

'The fact that Milbury doesn't appear in the Domesday Book.'

Adam thought for a minute. 'Yes, that is odd. There must have been a thriving community here in 1086.'

'Exactly.' Margaret sipped her drink, but her eyes never left Adam's face.

Hendrick loomed above them, carrying two glasses, one of which he handed to Adam.

'Excuse me, Margaret, but I'd like to borrow Adam back for a moment. I want him to meet Miss Clegg.'

He turned, to reveal a tall, angular woman standing behind him. 'Miss Clegg's the schoolteacher,' he said to Adam. 'I thought you might like to have a word with her about Matthew.'

Adam got to his feet. 'Oh yes. We've had some correspondence. Nice to meet you, Miss Clegg.'

Miss Clegg simpered girlishly. 'And you, Professor. It will be a privilege to teach the son of such an eminent man.'

'You may not consider it such a privilege when you hear his French. It's as bad as mine.'

'Oh, I expect he'll make up for it in the sciences.'

'I hope so. He's pretty advanced for his age.'

Miss Clegg glanced at Hendrick, and Adam intercepted a look of... what? Triumph? Satisfaction? It was hard to tell.

She turned back to him. 'When may I expect him?'

'Tomorrow. He's already missed three days of term. If he misses any more, he'll find it difficult to catch up.'

Hendrick patted him on the arm. 'Tomorrow, then. I'll arrange for someone to show him the way.'

'Thank you.'

Adam knew he should be feeling grateful to Hendrick, but for some reason he resented it. He realised he was being unreasonable – the man obviously meant well – but he couldn't help himself. Perhaps he just liked being independent. Or perhaps it was that conspiratorial look between Hendrick and Miss Clegg. Why should they have been so pleased to learn that his son was good at science?

CHAPTER THREE

HENDRICK WAS AS GOOD as his word. Next day, when Matthew left the cottage weighed down by a breakfast of eggs, gherkins, and chocolate cake, Bob was waiting for him.

Matthew smiled. This time, he would get in first.

'Happy Day,' he called.

Surprisingly, Bob didn't respond. He stared at him for a moment, looking puzzled.

'You're not supposed to…' He stopped abruptly.

'Not supposed to what?'

'Nothing. Come on. Mustn't be late on your first day.'

They cycled off, speeding through the narrow, winding streets to the edge of the village.

The schoolhouse was an old, converted rectory, with thick, diamond-patterned windows. Compared with Matthew's school, a modern, airy building, it looked dark and forbidding.

Inside, however, the atmosphere was cosy and informal: more like a large sitting-room than a schoolroom. On one side, at a long, polished table, most of the class sat silently waiting for the arrival of the teacher. On the other, three or four children sat at makeshift desks composed of armchairs and coffee tables, noisily throwing paper darts at each other. The contrast between the two groups was startling.

Bob pointed to one of the desks on the noisy side of the room.

'You should sit there for the moment.' He moved off to an empty chair at the long table.

Matthew noticed Sandra, the girl who had kept staring at him the day before, among the rowdy group.

As hers was the only face he recognised, he started to walk toward her. But then the ground under his feet suddenly seemed to move, and before he knew what was happening, he found himself full-length on the floor. He looked around, dazed and bewildered.

One of the dart-throwing boys was grinning down at him. A cheeky face, not unfriendly. 'So, new boy – what are you going to do about *that?*'

Matthew knew exactly what to do about it. He had had to take the same sort of action many times before.

'Break your leg,' he said cheerfully.

He grabbed the boy's foot and twisted, bringing him crashing to the floor. Before he had time to recover, Matthew was on top of him, pinioning his arms.

The boy heaved, threw Matthew sideways, and grabbed his hair. Matthew punched him in the stomach, and grabbed him around the waist. They rolled over and over, each trying to gain a decisive hold.

'STOP IT. BOTH OF YOU.' The voice was full of authority, and the two boys released each other, startled.

Sandra was looking down at them with contempt.

'You ought to be ashamed of yourselves. Specially you, Kevin. Attacking him the moment he walks through the door.'

Kevin picked himself up and dusted his trousers. 'I was just testing.'

'Testing what?'

'To see if he was human.'

Sandra frowned. 'Of course he's human. He only arrived yesterday.'

'Good. One of us, then.'

He turned, offered his hand to Matthew, and pulled him to his feet. 'Sorry about that. But we had to be sure.'

Matthew rubbed his bruised elbow. 'Sure of what?'

'That you weren't one of them.' Kevin jerked his head, indicating the group around the table. They were sitting as still as statues and as quiet as mice.

Matthew stared at the row of expressionless faces. 'One of them?'

'Don't be silly, Kevin,' Sandra broke in quickly. 'He doesn't know the difference.'

She and Kevin took their places at their improvised desks. Matthew slowly followed suit, wondering what on earth they had been talking about. He hadn't understood a word.

As he sat down, the door opened and Miss Clegg entered. She looked around, smiling. 'Happy Day, children.'

There was a chorus from the group at the table. 'Happy Day, Miss Clegg.' Matthew noticed that Sandra, Kevin, and the boy sitting next to him did not join in.

Miss Clegg moved behind her desk. 'Now before we begin, I would like you to welcome a new member of the class. Stand up, Matthew.'

Reluctantly, Matthew got to his feet. The children at the table were looking at him with polite interest, as if he were an insect under a microscope.

'This is Matthew Brake,' Miss Clegg went on, 'who is joining us for a few weeks. Matthew's father is an astrophysicist. Anyone know what that involves?'

Bob's hand shot up. 'Yes, Bob?'

'The study of matter and energy in relation to the stars, miss.'

Miss Clegg turned to Matthew, still smiling. 'Correct, Matthew?'

'Yes, miss.'

'Good. You can sit down now.'

Matthew sat back in his armchair, grateful that he was no longer the centre of attention.

Miss Clegg clasped her hands behind her back and walked slowly forward till she was standing in front of Sandra's desk.

'Anyone have any problems with the work I set you yesterday?' Three hands went up – Sandra, Kevin, and the fat boy next to him, who looked as if he had problems with everything.

Miss Clegg didn't seem at all surprised. 'Bob,' she called. 'Would you show us how you solved it?'

Bob crossed to the blackboard and wrote down the most complicated mathematical equation Matthew had ever seen. He was very good at figures, having been well taught by his father, but this was way beyond his reach. He watched with amazement and admiration as Bob resolved the problem quickly and efficiently, the chalk flying across the blackboard. It was an incredible feat for someone of his age.

Matthew turned, to find Sandra watching him intently. 'How do you explain *that?*' she seemed to be saying, obviously sharing his bewilderment.

Bob finished the equation and sat down, an expression of quiet satisfaction on his face. It wasn't arrogance or conceit: just pride at a job well done.

Kevin looked sourly at the long series of symbols on the blackboard and let out a loud raspberry. He for one didn't seem impressed.

Miss Clegg ignored him. She walked up to the blackboard and wiped it clean. 'Now I must look after our other friends,' she announced to the group at the table, 'so here's something else to be thinking about.'

She wrote down another equation, which Matthew found just as impossible to understand. But the group at the table seemed to have no such difficulty. They bent over their exercise books and began to work industriously.

Matthew copied down the figures and stared at them. An equation, he knew, was a statement of equality between known and unknown quantities. But what happened when they were *all* unknown quantities? How did you begin?

He put up his hand. 'Miss Clegg…'

Miss Clegg moved to peer over his shoulder. 'Not you, Matthew. We'll start you on something else, shall we? Just to see how you get on? Some of us even have difficulty with the simple stuff, don't we, Sandra?'

Sandra frowned. 'Yes, miss.'

Miss Clegg turned to the boy next to Kevin and ruffled his hair.

'What about you, Jimmo? No good asking to see your book, I suppose?' She picked up his exercise book and leafed through it, shaking her head sadly. 'No. Figures are not your strong point, are they, Jimmo? I don't suppose you could even tell me what one and one make?'

A crafty smile spread over Jimmo's plump face. 'Me dad's a farmer, miss,' he said unexpectedly.

Miss Clegg looked taken aback. 'What's that got to do with it?'

'I'll probably follow him, miss.'

'So?'

'Well… on a farm… put one and one together, and you usually get a third.'

Kevin hooted with laughter, curling up in his armchair.

Miss Clegg surveyed him coolly.

'You find that funny, Kevin?'

Kevin stopped laughing, sat up straight, and bit his lip nervously. 'Sorry, miss.'

Miss Clegg contemplated him in silence for a moment, then walked over and picked up his exercise book.

'Nothing to laugh about *here*, is there? Seems we've drawn another blank.' She moved back to Matthew and laid the open exercise book on his desk. 'Think you can do better, Matthew?'

Matthew looked at the figures with relief. Here was something he could understand: a simple equation he could solve without too much difficulty. He felt like a ship, back in harbour after sailing on uncharted seas.

He set to work, his logical mind taking him easily from step to step until the answer emerged, a golden nugget of truth. Wordlessly, he handed the book back to Miss Clegg.

She glanced at it and nodded, obviously pleased. 'Well done. I can see it won't take you long to catch up.'

'Catch up?'

'With the others.'

Matthew looked doubtfully at the children at the 'High Table.' 'Dunno about that, miss. I think they're a bit above my standard.'

'At the moment perhaps. But there's no knowing what you'll achieve once you've...' She stopped abruptly, as if she had already said too much.

Matthew waited for her to continue, but she made no effort to complete the sentence. 'Once I've what, miss?' he prompted.

'Once you've settled down.'

He had the feeling that was not what she was going to say, but before he could question her further, she had moved away.

'Anyone finished?' she asked, addressing the clever group.

A forest of hands shot up. Kevin groaned. And when Matthew turned, he again found Sandra's eyes on him. He had never met anyone who stared so much.

When Adam arrived at the Museum, he found Margaret typing at her desk, near a stack of filing cabinets. All around her were glass cases, filled with fossils and relics of every description: pieces of rock, flint, and pottery, all neatly labelled. On the walls were several maps and photographs, showing how Milbury had developed from a primitive settlement to a twentieth-century village. Behind the desk was a reproduction of the artist's drawing in the guidebook.

'Good morning.' Adam picked his way through the maze of exhibits, wondering how she would reply.

Margaret took off the horn-rimmed spectacles she was wearing and smiled. 'Good morning.'

'Not "Happy Day"?'

'Definitely not.'

'Thank heavens for that. It's getting on my nerves.'

Her smile faded. 'And you've only been here twenty-four hours. Wait till you've been here a week.'

She replaced her spectacles and began to type again, banging the keys savagely. Adam had to shout to make himself heard.

'Sounds more like a password than a greeting.'

She paused, glancing up at him over the top of her glasses. 'Yes.' This was said with such emphasis that Adam was convinced she was trying to convey some message to him. He waited for her to continue, but she seemed to think she had made herself clear. She returned to the typewriter, bashing at the machine as if it had insulted her.

Adam watched her for a moment, then moved away and started to wander around the room, studying the various charts on the walls. There was one that looked particularly intriguing. It was a large-scale Ordnance Survey map of the area, showing the village and the Stone Circle. A network of lines had been drawn on it, radiating out from the Circle like the spokes of a wheel.

Behind him, the sound of the typewriter suddenly stopped. 'Know what those are?'

Adam peered at the map. 'No.'

'Leylines.'

He turned and stared at her in astonishment. He knew all about leylines: invisible cables that were supposed to connect places of ancient sanctity. He had always dismissed the theory as being the invention of a few lunatics with more imagination than sense. And Margaret certainly didn't seem to fit into that category.

'Don't tell me you believe in all that mumbo-jumbo?'

Her face was impassive. 'I try to keep an open mind.'

'Oh, come on. Lines connecting churches, markstones, barrows, and so on?'

'And stone circles.'

So she was serious. He would have to tread carefully; he didn't want to offend her. 'My idea of hell.' He smiled, trying to lighten the atmosphere. 'Write out a hundred leylines.'

But there was no answering smile. 'I take it you're not a believer?' she said coolly.

Adam sighed. There was nothing for it: if their relationship was to develop, he would have to be honest.

'I'm a scientist,' he said quietly. 'Scientists need proof.'

'I can't offer you that, I'm afraid.' She rose, and crossed over to join him, staring thoughtfully at the map. 'There are some interesting theories, though.'

'Tell me.'

'Well, some people believe that the sacred places along these lines are temples, built as storehouses of psychic energy by Neolithic Man.'

This was too much. She was an extremely attractive woman, but Adam could no longer hide his scepticism.

'So Milbury's full of psychic energy, is it?'

She glanced at him, then looked quickly away, as if ashamed of her gullibility. 'It's full of *something*.'

He had no idea what she was talking about, but he decided not to press her further. If she chose to believe that the village was the centre of some Neolithic grid system, then nothing he could say would change her mind. He tried another tack.

'Who traced all these lines?'

'Various ley-hunters. There are people who spend all their spare time looking for them. Some I worked out for myself.'

'And how many are there?'

'Fifty-three.'

Adam frowned. 'That's interesting.'

'Why?'

'There are fifty-three standing stones left in the Circle.'

She turned to face him, gazing solemnly into his eyes. 'You think that's a coincidence?'

They were back on dangerous ground. It was time to change the subject. 'How long have you been here?' he asked, wandering down the row of glass cases.

Margaret, too, seemed glad to avoid an argument.

'Seems like ages,' she said, moving briskly back to her desk and putting the cover on the typewriter, 'but it's hardly been any time at all actually. A month, six weeks.'

'First time you've curated, is it?'

'First time I've had to earn my own living.' She stood for a minute, lost in her own thoughts; then, as if to dismiss any suggestion of self-pity, she produced a bright smile. 'Luckily, I had a degree in archaeology, so when my husband died I had some sort of qualification to fall back on.'

Adam sat on the edge of her desk. 'And do you enjoy the work?'

'The work? Oh yes…' Again, the suggestion of something left unsaid.

'So what aren't you enjoying?'

She sat down, picked up a pencil, and started to play with it, turning it over and over with nervous fingers.

'I don't enjoy being alone.'

Adam sensed her need. He, too, had experienced loneliness in the two years since his wife had died.

'Of course not,' he said sympathetically. 'When you lose someone… someone who's been part of you…'

'You don't understand.' She dropped the pencil and sat forward, her tone suddenly sharp and urgent. 'You haven't been here long enough.'

Adam frowned. 'You mean the natives are unfriendly?'

'I mean… I'm glad you're here.'

She stretched out her hand and he took it, surprised at the desperation in her voice. She seemed not so much lonely… as frightened.

'Adam,' she said softly, 'will you do something for me?'

'Of course.'

'Touch one of the stones.'

'Why?'

'I just want to see if you're the kind of man I think you are.'

The conversation was becoming so bizarre that Adam wanted to laugh. But her expression told him it was no laughing matter as far as she was concerned. He must continue to humour her. 'And what sort of man is that?' he asked.

She rose, tightened her grip on his hand, and started to pull him toward the door. 'Please… come with me. Please.'

Adam allowed himself to be dragged out of the Museum, wondering what on earth he was letting himself in for. Had he fallen into the clutches of the Madwoman of Milbury? If so, he decided he didn't mind all that much; he found her clutches decidedly pleasant…

School was over for the day, but Matthew still sat at his desk, watching the High Table children file quietly out of the classroom. They were so well-behaved, it was ridiculous. Not like any other kids he'd met. At his old school, there was absolute pandemonium as soon as the final bell rang. But for all the noise this lot made, they might have been monks who had taken vows of silence.

He stood up, collected his books together, and stowed them in his satchel.

'Come on,' said a voice from the doorway.

He looked up, to find Sandra waiting for him. 'What's the hurry?'

'Don't you want to get out of here?' She looked around the room with distaste. 'This place gives me the creeps.'

'Why?'

'Because of them, of course.' She jerked her head toward the empty chairs at the long table, turned, and marched out.

Matthew followed thoughtfully, conscious of a sense of relief as he walked through the door. He suddenly realised how oppressive the atmosphere inside the classroom had been.

A group of boys was clustered around the school bulletin board in the hall. Matthew peered over their heads to see what they were looking at.

'The football team,' Sandra explained. 'There's a match on Saturday.'

They were about to move on, when Kevin pushed his way from the centre of the group, blocking their path. His face was flushed with anger.

'I've been dropped,' he announced incredulously. 'She's actually had the nerve to drop me.'

Bob appeared at his elbow. 'What did you expect?' he asked softly.

'What did I expect?' Kevin whirled around on him, glad of someone on whom he could vent his wrath. 'I scored a hat-trick in the last match. I certainly didn't expect to be given the push.'

'You argued with the ref,' said Bob imperturbably. 'That's no way to be happy.'

Kevin snorted with derision. 'How could I be happy with that centre-back going for my legs all the time? And the ref took no notice.'

'Perhaps he was nearsighted.'

'Then he should wear contact lenses.'

Bob shrugged. 'Well, you told him what you thought of him. Did it make you feel better?'

Kevin raised his fist and held it in front of Bob's face. 'I'll tell you what *would* make me feel better…'

Bob didn't flinch. 'Go on, then. Thump me.'

Kevin's fist crashed into his chin. Bob staggered back, hit his head on the wall, and slumped to the ground. The boys drew back, forming a ring around the two contestants, and Matthew waited for the inevitable fight to begin. Bob was considerably bigger than Kevin, and if he really punched his weight it would be a massacre. But surprisingly, he made no effort to retaliate. He picked himself up, rubbed the back of his head, and grinned.

'You see?' he said pleasantly. 'Didn't solve anything, did it?'

He turned and walked away. Kevin, who had braced himself for battle, slowly lowered his fists. 'Chicken!' he called. 'Happy little chicken!'

'Don't be silly, Kevin,' said Sandra quietly. 'You know that's not true.'

Matthew stared at her. 'What *is* true?' he asked.

'He just doesn't believe in fighting. None of them do.'

'Why not?'

'Because it doesn't make them happy.'

They walked out into the yard, collected their bicycles, and set off side by side toward the village.

There were so many questions Matthew wanted to ask, but he got the impression that Sandra was as puzzled as he was. She seemed to be waiting for *him* to provide the answers.

He decided to cycle around the Stone Circle to see if his father had begun his field-work. He might be able to make himself useful, copying down the magnetometer readings.

'I'm going to take a look at the stones,' he said to Sandra as they reached the crossroads. 'See you tomorrow.'

She raised her arm in acknowledgement, and disappeared down the winding lane that led to the Museum. Matthew turned left, bent low over the handlebars, and started to pedal as fast as he could: the winner of the Tour de France approaching the finishing line in Paris...

As Adam and Margaret walked toward the stones, she told him what was known about them from the archaeological point of view.

'They're undressed sarsens,' she explained, 'weighing approximately forty tons each. There were a hundred in the original circle, of which fifty-three now remain. Two avenues of stone used to extend from the circle, one to the southeast, which terminates in the Linnet Barrow on the hill called the Hac-Pen or Serpent's Head, also known as the Sanctuary... and the other to the southwest, which no longer exists. These avenues form the head and tail of the Solar Serpent, the symbol of inner truth.'

Adam looked at her with undisguised admiration. 'Bravo!'

She smiled. 'Not bad for a beginner?'

'You're a walking encyclopedia.'

'Not really. I've just got a good memory.'

A grey shape loomed massively above them. Adam stopped, and stared up at it thoughtfully.

'Forty tons, eh? Wouldn't like to be caught under *that*.'

Margaret shuddered. 'Someone *was* caught, centuries ago. A barber-surgeon was helping to bury one of the stones, when it fell over and crushed him to death. His skeleton's in the Museum.'

'Poor chap. When was he found?'

'Earlier this century. They re-erected the sarsen, and there he was underneath.'

Adam tried to imagine what it must have been like to look up and realise for one horrifying split-second that the huge rock was about to fall… 'Why were they burying it?' he asked.

'Local superstition. The villagers believed that if they buried one of the stones each year, it would bring them luck.'

'Didn't do the barber-surgeon much good, did it?'

'No.' She put a hand on his arm. 'So when you start messing about out here, be careful.'

He laughed. 'Don't worry. I'll ask my son to keep watch for me.'

Her expression didn't change. 'What exactly do you intend to do?'

'Well, first of all… a bit of electronic dowsing. Try and find where the missing stones are.'

'You don't need to dowse.' She waved her hand toward the rest of the circle. 'There are concrete posts marking their positions.'

'I like to do my own research. And I like playing with expensive sonic equipment. Now… you said you wanted me to touch one of these things?'

'Yes.' She stepped back, as if expecting an explosion.

'Just… touch it?'

'That's right.'

He shrugged, stretched out his hand, and touched the rock… completely unprepared for the sudden, excruciating pain that shot up his arm, welding his hand to the stone. He shut his eyes and gritted his teeth, trying to break the contact, but it was no use. The pain seemed to pass through his whole body, transfixing him to the spot. He couldn't move, he couldn't think, he couldn't see…

Yes, he *could* see. He could see Matthew's picture, and it was as if the ring of shadowy figures had been shocked into life by the current. They were raising their arms in protection against the bright pillar of light in the centre, and turning to flee into the surrounding darkness.

He felt himself falling down and down into the same darkness… whirling around and around in a whirlpool of night. Then, at last, no pain. No sensation of any kind. Nothing.

CHAPTER FOUR

THE WINNER OF THE Tour de France was racing down the home stretch. On either side of him, enthusiastic crowds were cheering and waving their handkerchiefs. Who is this young English boy who has crossed the channel to beat the cream of European cyclists? Holder of the Yellow Jersey for ten consecutive days, he has looked unbeatable from the start. But where has he come from? Why was there no advance publicity about this incredible athlete?

Matthew was using the edge of the Circle as the finishing line. He made sure the road was clear, then bent almost double in an effort to put on a final spurt. If he could reach the line in another ten seconds, he would have beaten the existing record by half an hour. He watched the road flash past his front wheel as he began the countdown – ten, nine, eight, seven, six…

A pair of legs suddenly came into view six feet ahead. Dirty boots and tatty trousers in the middle of the road. Matthew jerked the handlebars to avoid the obstacle, and the bike toppled sideways, sending him flying into a hedge.

Winded, he lay still for a moment, wondering how many bones he'd broken. He didn't feel any pain yet, but he supposed that would come later. Cautiously, he moved one leg, then the other. Yes, they felt all right. And the arms. Perhaps it was his spine. No, he could sit up without difficulty. It seemed that, by some miracle, he hadn't hurt himself at all.

He crawled slowly out of the hedge, brambles tearing and clawing at his skin. His bike was lying in the middle of the road, the wheels still spinning. Next to it stood the dirty boots and tatty trousers.

He looked up at the man's face. Lined, weatherbeaten, and as cunning as a weasel. Blue eyes were staring down at him with hypnotic intensity. No hint of apology. Challenging.

'Well? Anything to say, boy?' The voice had a harsh Welsh lilt to it.

Matthew didn't reply. He had suddenly noticed the telescope protruding from the pocket of the torn raincoat.

The man growled, apparently disappointed. He wheeled around and started to shuffle off down the road.

Matthew suddenly found his voice and called after him. 'Hey! You... NUTTER!'

The man turned and looked at him speculatively, like an old crow contemplating a worm. 'Go on, then.'

'What do you mean, go on? Look what you've done to my bike, you clumsy oaf! Look at my clothes!'

To his surprise, the man grinned from ear to ear and shuffled back toward him. 'That's better. Go on, have a bit of a swear. Call me words.'

Matthew picked up his bike. 'If you've damaged my bike, I'll do more than that. I'll wrap what's left of it around your scrawny neck.'

He pushed it around in a circle. One of the brake pads was catching on the front wheel, but apart from that, everything seemed to be in order.

The man watched him, still grinning. 'Should have looked where you were going, eh?'

Matthew scowled. '*I* should have looked where I was going? What about you? Blind people shouldn't be moving around the countryside without their white sticks and guide dogs.'

A rasping sound came from the man's throat, like sandpaper on wood, and Matthew realised that he was actually laughing. It really was quite amazing: the more you insulted him, the more he seemed to enjoy it. Perhaps he was the village idiot.

'What's so funny?'

'A young lad with spirit, that's what's funny.'

'Why?'

'Someone who can still think for himself. That's rare, that is. What's your name, boy?'

'Matthew.'

The piercing blue eyes came nearer, and a bony hand descended on his shoulder. 'Friends are few and far between in these parts, Matthew. If you should ever need one, go to the Sanctuary and wait. Dai will know it. Dai will find you there…'

With that, he turned, and disappeared into the undergrowth. Matthew stared after him, completely at a loss. Instinctively, he knew that this tattered scarecrow of a man wished him well, that he was indeed a friend. But who was he? Where had he come from? And what was it about Matthew's anger that had seemed to please him so much?

Who, where, and what? Three questions that one seemed to be constantly asking in Milbury. Which meant there was a fourth, and that was – why?

When Matthew returned to the cottage, he found his father flat out on the sofa. His eyes were closed and he looked very pale. A red-haired woman was bending over him, holding a glass of water.

'Adam,' she was calling softly, 'Adam…'

Matthew started forward in concern. 'Dad…'

The woman glanced up and put a finger to her lips. 'Don't worry,' she whispered. 'He'll be all right in a minute.'

Matthew stared at her. 'What happened?'

'Good question.' His father's eyes flicked open, and he slowly hauled himself up into a sitting position. He blinked around at the woman. 'What *did* happen?'

'You don't remember my helping you back there? Well, *I* remember. You nearly broke my shoulder.'

Adam managed a weak grin. 'And they say the age of chivalry is dead. By the way, have you two introduced yourselves? My son Matthew. Margaret Smythe, the Curator of the Museum.'

Sandra's mother. Yes, there was a strong resemblance. Matthew grinned. His father had certainly wasted no time.

'I'm sorry,' Margaret was saying. 'It was very stupid of me. But I'd no idea the reaction would be so violent.' She offered Adam the glass of water. 'Here.'

Adam scowled and pushed her hand away. 'This is no time for a bath. You'll find some Scotch in that cupboard.'

He buried his head in his hands. Margaret crossed over to the sideboard and poured a large drink.

'It was my fault,' she explained to Matthew. 'I took him out to the Circle and asked him to touch one of the stones.'

Matthew frowned. 'Why?'

'To see if I was the sort of man she thought I was,' said Adam. 'What did that mean?'

Margaret moved back to the sofa and handed him a glass. 'A man of… sensitivity.'

'Sensitivity to what?'

She looked embarrassed. 'Soon after I arrived here, I read a fringe-lunatic's book about residual energy in standing stones. A psychic force that only certain people – perceptives, the writer called them – could feel. Well, I touched that same stone, and I thought I felt something. A slight shock. But nothing like the shock it must have given you.'

Adam sipped his drink thoughtfully. 'That wasn't psychic force. It was…'

'Electromagnetic energy,' Matthew broke in.

'Exactly. A perfectly natural phenomenon.'

Margaret stared at him. 'Even though you were grounded? And so was the stone?'

'There's probably some simple explanation.'

'There is.'

'What?'

'Psychic forces don't obey the same laws as electromagnetic ones.'

Adam put down his glass and stood up. 'Oh come on, Margaret. There's nothing psychic about residual magnetism. Ask Matt: he'll tell you. You don't need special powers to receive a common or garden electric shock.'

She smiled. 'Hardly common or garden. You flew through the air with the greatest of ease.'

'Yes.' Adam looked puzzled. 'There's certainly a great deal of energy there. I can't wait to…'

He stopped abruptly, as his eye fell on the painting. For a moment, he looked as though he was going to pass out again, and Matthew started forward in alarm. The movement seemed to snap his father out of his reverie, and to draw his attention to Matthew's dishevelled appearance.

'Matt! What happened?'

'Nothing much, dad. Just fell off my bike.'

'Hurt yourself?'

'No.'

'Well be careful. I've got no use for an assistant with a broken leg.'

Matthew tried to look equally stern. 'And I've got no use for an employer who keeps fainting all the time.'

Margaret laughed and took both their arms. 'That's what I've been missing,' she announced gaily. 'People who are *really* happy.'

That night, over supper, Adam told Matthew exactly what had happened: of the shock he had felt when he touched the stone, and of the strange visions he had seen. He pooh-poohed Margaret's suggestion that some sort of psychic force might have been responsible, but could offer no rational interpretation. Residual magnetism could be measured, but he had never heard of anyone who had actually *felt* it. And energy so powerful that it caused hallucinations! There was no scientific principle to explain *that* away.

Matthew hadn't told his father about the disappearing lorry, because the whole thing sounded so absurd. And he knew exactly what Adam would say: to see things that weren't there was a sign of overtiredness. He ought to get more sleep, go to bed earlier, etc. etc. The whole heavy parent bit.

But now, owing to Adam's own puzzling experience, he had a comeback. So he recounted the episode with Bob as objectively as he could, reliving the terror he had felt when a fatal accident had seemed inevitable, and the relief when he realised that Bob was unharmed.

Adam listened attentively. He seemed convinced that the lorry had not been a figment of Matthew's imagination, dismissing the suggestion that it might have been an optical illusion.

'But you *heard* it. Mirages don't usually come in full stereo.'

'Well?' Matthew was stuffing himself with Mrs Crabtree's delicious meringue. 'Any other ideas?'

Adam thought for a moment. 'Is there a bypass?'

'We didn't see one on the way in.'

'Perhaps we were distracted by the stones.'

But Matthew was sure there wasn't a bypass. And next day, after school, he cycled out to the edge of the Circle to check. Yes, he was right. The road stretched away between the avenues of stones, and there was no turn the lorry could have taken. No way it could have avoided passing through the village.

He found Adam farther around the perimeter of the Circle, working with his magnetometer. He seemed preoccupied with the readings he was getting, and when Matthew told him of his discovery, merely grunted. There was obviously something more important in his mind.

Matthew wandered around one of the stones, awed by its sheer size. There must be at least as much of it below ground as there was above. Incredible to think that primitive man had possessed the technology to lift it.

He stood back and looked at the stone through narrowed eyes. It seemed to be leaning slightly, but the distribution of its mass was so uneven that it was impossible to tell how much. He wandered over to the next stone, and found the same problem: it was such an odd shape, one would need a theodolite to determine its plumb-line.

A theodolite. Perhaps he could make one. Adam had a book called *How Things Work*, and if he could assemble the necessary components... Yes. He'd look it up when he got home, to find out exactly what he needed.

Suddenly, behind him, he heard a sound that made him catch his breath: a high-pitched, plaintive scream.

He whirled around and listened, turning his head sideways into the breeze. There it was again, a thin screech, full of fear and desperation. It came from behind the next stone.

He ran over to it and looked down. A rabbit was hopping frantically backwards and forwards, its hind leg caught in a wire snare. The animal was plainly terrified, and at the sight of Matthew it redoubled its efforts to free itself.

Matthew bent down and inspected the snare, trying to discover the best way to release the captive without harming it. He pulled the whole contraption out of the ground, and carefully loosened the wire noose, holding the rabbit tightly so that it wouldn't break its leg in its struggle to get away. Then he set it gently on the grass, and it scuttled off, its white tail bobbing, until it disappeared over the high, circular earthwork just outside the stones.

Matthew watched it go, then turned his attention to the snare. It was obviously a home-made job, efficient but crude. He was about to destroy it, when a thought occurred to him. This was a poacher's trap, belonging to someone who came and went as he pleased, someone independent of the rest of the community. And he knew a man who fitted that description. Dai.

Now Dai had a telescope. And a telescope had lenses. Matthew had a small reflector-telescope of his own, but the lenses were quite unsuitable for a theodolite. Dai's, however, would be perfect.

Matthew searched in his pockets, found a scrap of paper and the stub of a pencil, and drew a picture of a broken bicycle. Then he rolled up the paper, placed it in the wire noose, replaced the trap where he had found it, and covered it with grass.

He stood up and regarded his handiwork with satisfaction. That should fetch him.

And fetch him it did. The following evening, Matthew was alone at the cottage putting together a collection of bits and pieces that had begun to look something like the theodolite in the textbook, when there was a tap at the window.

Matthew looked around, startled. Dai was outside, holding the drawing of the bicycle pressed against the windowpane.

Matthew ran to the door and opened it. 'Come in,' he called.

Dai materialised out of the darkness, and peered at him like a wary ferret. 'What do you want?' he asked suspiciously.

'I need your help.'

'Why?'

'Come in, and I'll tell you.'

'No fear.' Dai held up the drawing. 'Was it you? Left this in my snare?'

Matthew smiled. 'Yes. Seemed a good idea to use it as a postbox.'

'You let my supper go?'

'I left you an invitation instead.'

He took hold of the old man's arm and pulled him inside. Dai stood just inside the door, grumbling to himself. 'Can't eat invitations,' he said crossly. 'Rabbit. That's what I fancied tonight. Nice piece of coney. And you had to let it go.'

Matthew dragged him into the room. 'Never mind,' he said soothingly. 'There's plenty of…'

But Dai wasn't listening. 'Pigeon,' he was saying. 'Set a net for pigeon. Or rooks. That's it. Rooks.' He turned and made for the door.

'How about a piece of chicken?' Matthew called after him. 'Tomatoes. Bread and cheese. Fruit.'

Dai stopped in his tracks and glanced back. For the first time, he noticed a mouth-watering selection of dishes laid out on the table. A crafty expression spread over his face. 'Got a bit of cider?' he enquired, licking his lips.

Matthew waved at the bottles on the sideboard. 'Help yourself.'

Dai made a beeline for one of the bottles, tore the top off it, and drank deeply. Then, wiping his mouth on the sleeve of his filthy raincoat, he carried the bottle to the table and helped himself to a chicken leg. 'Where's your dad?' he asked, tearing into the chicken like a wild animal.

'At the Museum. Picking up some geological surveys. That's his story, anyway.' Matthew knew that his father had only used the surveys as an excuse: he'd worn his green anorak – a sure sign that he wanted to impress a lady.

'Some sort of scientist, they tell me.' Dai was wolfing down food as if he hadn't eaten for a year. His eye fell on the makeshift theodolite. 'What's that, then? A theodolite?'

'What do you know about theodolites?'

'I know you need a plane-table.'

Matthew produced the table he had constructed that afternoon on Adam's camera tripod: a plywood plate and two small spirit-levels. He clipped the theodolite onto it and stood back proudly.

If Dai was impressed, he didn't show it. He stared at his chicken leg with distaste. 'Who cooked this thing?'

'Mrs Crabtree. Why? What's wrong with it?'

'How should I know? I'm not a doctor. But it's certainly dead: I'll say that for it.'

Matthew sat down opposite him. 'Know anything about surveying?'

'Tell her next time… a bit of tarragon under the skin. And an old potato inside, to keep it moist.'

'Well, do you?'

Dai stopped eating for a moment. 'Yes. That is, if I haven't forgotten. Used to be a miner, see?'

'A coal miner?'

'Coal, silver, gold. I've dug for everything in my time. Dug holes in the water for fish, I have. Dug holes in the earth for bones.' His blue eyes rested on the theodolite. 'What do you want to survey?'

Matthew shrugged. 'The stones.'

'It's been done,' said Dai sharply. 'Don't meddle.' He stood up and began stuffing apples into his pockets. 'Got any nuts?'

'No.'

'Pity.' He opened his raincoat and stuck a couple of bananas into his belt.

'The thing is, Dai,' Matthew went on, 'the stones all seem to be leaning slightly toward the centre. My father reckons it's probably weathering or subsidence, but I was wondering if they all lean at the same angle.'

The old man turned to face him. 'And if they do?'

'I don't know. But it'd be interesting, wouldn't it?'

'Just nosy, eh? Take my advice, boy. Leave the stones alone.' He loped across the room toward the door. Matthew followed him, and grabbed his arm.

'It couldn't be coincidence, could it? If they do all lean at the same angle?'

Dai stared down at him. 'And if they don't? If your father's right? What then?'

Matthew grinned ruefully. 'Want to buy a home-made theodolite? One careful owner…'

Dai looked thoughtfully across at the plane-table.

'How're you going to finish off that sight-machine?'

'Well, that's where I need your help. If I could borrow the lenses from your telescope…'

'Oh no.' Dai took his telescope from his pocket and hugged it protectively. 'No chance of that, boy. None at all.'

'It'd only be for a couple of days,' said Matthew patiently, 'and I'd take great care of them. You see, there are a lot of important figures my father and I have to collect. And the only way I'm going to get this particular set is if you help me.'

The old man hesitated, then thrust the telescope into his hands. 'All right. But only for a day or two, mind.'

'Thanks. There's so much to do before we leave.'

'Leave?' The blue eyes opened wide in surprise. 'What do you mean? Leave the Circle? Leave Milbury?'

'Yes.'

'Leave the stones?' Dai shook his head, amused. 'You never will.'

Matthew frowned. 'What do you mean?'

'Nobody leaves the Circle.'

'Nonsense. You leave. You come and go as you please.'

'And where do I go, eh? The Avenue? The Sanctuary? The barrow? Never outside the stones. Never beyond their sight, boy. Never out of their grasp.'

He opened the door and stared out into the darkness, speaking in a harsh whisper. 'Nobody leaves the Circle. Not until the day of release...'

He disappeared into the night. Matthew stared after him, trying to make sense of the ominous warning he had left floating in the air. 'Nobody leaves the Circle,' he had said. How absurd! There was nothing to stop them. They would leave as soon as his father had finished his research, and that wouldn't be a moment too soon. This place, with its strange, puppet-like children and its potty old poachers, was beginning to get on his nerves.

The next weekend, Matthew took his theodolite down to the stones and started measuring their angles of inclination. These were so startling in their uniformity that he checked each one three times to make sure of its accuracy. In every case, the angle was the same: exactly ninety degrees.

He walked thoughtfully back to the cottage, wondering what his father would make of his discovery. It was quite extraordinary that after three thousand years, there had not even been one degree of subsidence anywhere.

Adam, however, was busy with his own research, correlating the figures in his notebook with various surveys and geological reports that littered the table. He looked up as Matthew entered, obviously excited.

'Hello, Matt. Come and look at this.' He was waving a printout from one of his machines.

Matthew took the chart and studied it. His father had taught him how to interpret the figures, and they didn't seem to reveal anything particularly unusual.

He looked up. 'Rock?'

'That's right.'

'So?'

'The whole Circle seems to have a rock base to it. But the interesting thing is… there's no rock in the area.'

Matthew frowned. 'That's odd.'

'And there's something else.' Adam picked up his notebook. 'The rock base has a definite declivity toward the centre. It's as if there were some sort of giant dish under the ground, with the stones marking its perimeter.'

'A rock dish? And there's no record of it? No one seems to have spotted it before?'

'Well, the geological reports for this area don't go all that far back. By the time they started drilling hereabouts, I imagine the authorities had the Circle well protected. The only way we'd be allowed to go this deep is with our sonics.'

Matthew thought for a moment. 'How about alignment?' he asked. 'Have you got any further with that?'

'No.' Adam flopped down in a chair, put his hands behind his head, and stared at the ceiling. 'And that's another mystery. Most megalithic circles are aligned to the sun, right? Either summer or winter solstice, or both. Stonehenge, for instance, is aligned for both solar and lunar predictions. But this one isn't.'

'What about the other planets? A major star, perhaps?'

Adam shook his head wearily. 'There's no obvious alignment. You can check my calculations if you like.'

But Matthew had never known his father to make a mistake with his figures. He wandered over to the window, and gazed out toward the Circle. A crow was sitting on top of the nearest stone, a dark silhouette against the evening sky. 'Puzzle, puzzle,' he said softly.

'Exactly. No circle was ever constructed at random.'

Matthew turned. 'Well, I'm afraid I've come up against a dead end too. You remember I thought the stones seemed to be leaning?'

'Yes.'

'Well, they aren't.'

Adam stared at him. 'What do you mean?'

'I mean I was wrong. The stones are dead upright. Every one of them at a ninety-degree angle to the ground.'

'Oh come on. You can't rely on that ramshackle machine of yours.'

'Yes, I can. It may be ramshackle, but it can measure just as accurately as a proper theodolite.'

'And you measured *all* the stones?'

'Twenty-three of them. I gave up after that.'

Adam stood up and began to pace around the room.

'All pointing in one precise direction – upwards. Yes, that may be it.' He stopped and ruffled Matthew's hair. 'Matt, I think it's just possible you may have cracked it...'

CHAPTER FIVE

DURING THE NEXT FEW days, Adam and Matthew carefully checked each other's findings. For Matthew, the work was a relief after struggling all day with the problems Miss Clegg set him. She seemed pleased with his progress, not at all worried that he was still so far behind the geniuses at the High Table. She kept assuring him that he would soon catch up.

Compared with Sandra, Kevin and Jimmo, however, it was Matthew who was the genius. They were as far behind him as he was behind the others, so that he found himself in a group of one, halfway between knowledge and ignorance. And he knew which he preferred. If knowledge turned one into a smirking zombie, then give him happy ignorance every time.

When Adam asked him how he was getting on at school, he'd been deliberately non-committal. He didn't want to worry his father while he was so busy with his research, and in any case, what could he say? That some of the kids were so much cleverer than he? That they always did as they were told, and never did anything wrong? Adam would wonder what he was complaining about.

So he continued to do the best he could, ignoring the complicated equations which the bright children seemed to solve with such ease, and concentrating on the problems that were within his reach. And as time went on, these became progressively more difficult, taxing his considerable ability to the utmost.

He was always glad to get home. Tired and hungry, he would dive into Mrs Crabtree's teas with gusto; then, carrying a triple-decker sandwich up to his bedroom, would sit for hours at his desk, poring over his father's astronomical charts, trying to solve the mystery of the Stone Circle's non-alignment.

For Adam had been right. The Circle appeared to have no connection with any known celestial body. Yet it must have been constructed for a purpose: other circles, such as Stonehenge, proved that Neolithic Man's knowledge of mathematics was astonishingly advanced. What, then, was the purpose of the Milbury Ring?

Matthew's pride and joy was a small reflector-telescope, which his father had given him for his last birthday. He had set it up at his bedroom window, and night after night he would gaze up at the sky, scanning it section by section, searching for some uncharted star to which the Circle might be aligned. But it was a forlorn hope. Everything visible would surely have been plotted years ago.

Since Adam had hinted that Matthew might unwittingly have solved the problem, he had remained strangely secretive. When Matthew had asked him *what* he was supposed to have solved, his father had refused to answer, promising to let him know as soon as he had checked all the stones. So Matthew had no alternative but to conduct his own research, which was leading him precisely nowhere.

Sometimes, after school, he would accompany Sandra back to the Museum. He found it a fascinating place, and with Margaret always ready to explain the various maps and charts, he had learned a great deal about Milbury's history. He was particularly intrigued by the leylines, which Adam dismissed as so much hogwash. But that was the trouble with scientists: they weren't interested in unsubstantiated theories. And Matthew was convinced that science couldn't provide all the answers. So he'd made his own copy of the leyline-map and hung it on his bedroom wall above his desk.

One evening, as he was browsing around the Museum, Adam appeared. He looked tired but exhilarated, as if his investigations had at last borne fruit.

'Send this telegram for me, would you, Matt?' he said, handing him a scrap of paper and a five-pound note. 'And make it Express.'

Matthew glanced at the address. 'Mount Palomar Observatory, eh?'

Adam grinned. 'That's right.'

'You found the answer, then?'

'I think so. Or rather *you* have.'

Margaret rose from her desk to join them. 'The answer to what?'

'Come here, and I'll show you.' Adam took her arm and guided her to the glass case that contained the model of the village. Matthew followed, peering over his shoulder. 'A few days ago, Matt made an interesting discovery. He found that every one of these stones was upright: I mean, geometrically upright, at an angle of precisely ninety degrees.'

Margaret looked puzzled. 'So what does that prove?'

'It doesn't *prove* anything. But it suggests an interesting possibility – so interesting that I thought it was worth making a thorough check. It's taken me all this time to complete it.'

'All right. Let's have it.'

Adam bent over the glass case and stared thoughtfully at the model. 'I think it's possible – only possible, mind – that this Circle is aligned *upwards*. If the stone dish underneath it was designed as a receiver for those psychic forces of yours, then it follows that the signals must come from a source directly *above...*'

'Sounds a bit far-fetched,' said Margaret doubtfully. 'No other circle is aligned like that.'

'I know. But the fact that there's been no subsidence at all for five thousand years must mean that the stones are socketed into the rock. Which suggests that the angle was of paramount importance.'

Matthew whistled softly. 'So it could be a kind of primitive Jodrell Bank? Immovably aligned with… something up there.'

'That's right.'

'But what?'

Adam shrugged. 'I'm hoping Mount Palomar can tell us. There's nothing charted on the alignment path.'

'Nothing?' Margaret stared at him incredulously.

'Nothing visible.'

'Then there goes your theory. I simply can't believe that a Neolithic Archpriest designed all this to do *nothing*.'

'No. But it's just conceivable there could be some obscure power source up there.'

'That might be best left alone.'

Adam shook his head, smiling. 'Where would science be if we stopped asking questions? Go on, Matt. The sooner we send those co-ordinates off, the sooner we'll know the answer.'

'How long will it take them, dad? To check the alignment path?'

'Not long. If there's anything there, it'll be catalogued.'

Matthew ran out, climbed onto his bike, and raced through the village to the Post Office. He arrived, breathless, just as Mrs Warner was closing up for the day.

She stood in the doorway, beaming down at him: by now, Matthew was a regular customer. 'Just in time,' she said, her eyes twinkling behind her thick glasses. 'Another minute, and you'd have missed your ice cream.'

'It's not an ice cream, Mrs Warner,' panted Matthew. 'It's a telegram.'

'A telegram, eh? Must be important, then. Come inside.'

She moved behind the small window at the back of the shop. 'Now then. Have you got the message all written down?'

'Yes.' Matthew slid the piece of paper under the window.

Mrs Warner read the words carefully, her smile gradually fading. 'You can't send this, dear,' she said quietly.

'Why not?'

'It's to America. The USA.'

She was treating him like a child, and Matthew began to feel irritated. 'You don't expect me to send smoke signals, do you?'

'But it'll be expensive. Do you realise how much it would cost?'

He slapped the five-pound note down on the counter. 'This ought to cover it. And I'll have an ice lolly with the change.'

She picked up the note and stared at it as if it were forged. 'Very well, dear,' she said reluctantly. 'If you wait a moment, I'll tell you how much it comes to.'

She disappeared into a back room. Matthew frowned after her: what was it about these pleasant village women that made him dislike them so much? There was something... false about her: just as there was about Mrs Crabtree. He preferred people who let you know what they were thinking, even if they were surly and bad-tempered. But he couldn't stand this... this continual *pleasantness*. It was like a hard, smooth shell which was impossible to penetrate.

Only once had there been the slightest crack in the shell: and that had been when Mrs Warner read the telegram...

Matthew had carefully memorised the co-ordinates that Adam had worked out, and when he got back to his bedroom, he looked them up in his book of astronomical charts. But it was a fruitless search: the narrow strip of sky that passed directly over the Circle seemed to be completely empty.

He propped the book up on his desk and stared at it, disappointed. It just didn't make sense. If the Circle had been constructed with a consistent ninety-degree alignment, as his father had suggested, then there ought to be something there. Perhaps they were on the wrong track.

Adam poked his head round the door. 'Hi.'

Matthew grunted, still preoccupied with the chart. Adam moved up to stand behind him.

'The alignment path?'

'Uh-huh. Seems to be within the constellation of the Great Bear.'

'That's right.'

'And there's nothing there.'

'I told you.'

Matthew looked up at him. 'Could it be a void?'

'Unlikely. Had supper yet?'

'I had a sandwich.'

'Oh yes? What revolting mixture did you come up with this time?'

Matthew grinned. He enjoyed watching his father's taste-buds curl up. 'Ham and banana. With gherkins. And honey.'

'Ugh!'

'Well, you let me eat school dinners.'

Adam crossed over to sit on the bed. 'School. You don't talk much about that. How are you getting on?'

Matthew glanced at him and looked quickly away. 'All right,' he said edgily.

'I've made a few enquiries about Miss Clegg. Apparently she's a maths specialist. Should have thought that was right up your street.'

'Yes.'

'Not too difficult for you?'

'I can do the stuff she gives *me*.'

Adam frowned. 'So? What's wrong?'

'Nothing.'

'If you're finding it all too easy…'

'It's not that.'

'What then?'

Matthew stood up, crossed over to the window, and started fiddling with the knobs of his telescope. There was nothing for it: he would just have to try and explain…

'There seems to be two lots of kids,' he said, choosing his words carefully. 'Some are just… ordinary. And the others are…' He paused, searching for an accurate description.

'Extraordinary?'

'Yes.'

'In what way?'

Matthew turned and leaned on the windowsill. 'They're brilliant, dad. I mean, *really* brilliant. Some of them are younger than me, yet they're doing problems I can't even begin to understand.'

'Really?' Adam looked impressed.

'But there's something else. The brilliant ones are so... so quiet.'

'Compared with you, you mean?'

'No. Somehow, they don't behave like kids at all.'

'Because they're quiet?'

'Because they're not natural.'

Adam heaved himself off the bed and stretched. 'Well, I've heard some complaints in my time, but grumbling because your mates are too quiet is a new one. I wish I had the same cause for complaint.'

Matthew grinned. 'You'd be bored out of your mind.'

'Try me.' Adam suddenly noticed the leyline-map on the wall. 'What's that?'

'Leylines. I copied them from the map in the Museum, and replotted them slightly.'

'Why?'

'Because they interest me.'

'I've told you before. It's all a load of rubbish.'

Matthew crossed over to the map and unpinned it. 'It's a fascinating theory, though. That the circles are storehouses of psychic energy, connected by invisible cables in a worldwide grid system.'

Adam yawned. 'A theory is only fascinating to me if it's based on sound scientific principles.'

'Don't be so stuffy, dad. I want to show you something.' Matthew laid the map on his desk and picked up a pencil. 'Now apparently leylines never go *through* a point, but always touch it at a tangent.'

'Well?'

'These don't. Every one of them comes straight up to one of the stones and then stops.'

'How inconsiderate of them.'

'That's assuming the point they're supposed to be touching is the Circle. But what if it was much smaller? What if the actual power centre was *inside* the Circle?'

For the first time, Adam began to look interested. 'You mean, the geographical centre?'

'No. Watch.' Matthew picked up a ruler and projected three of the lines into the Circle. They formed a small triangle. 'I could have done that with any one of the lines, and the result would have been the same.'

Adam bent over the map and peered closely at it. 'There's a house inside that triangle. Highfield House.'

'Yes.' Matthew circled it with his pencil. 'Wonder who it belongs to.'

'I'll ask Margaret,' said Adam, making for the door. 'I promised to take her to the pub tonight.'

Matthew grinned at him. ' 'Ello, 'ello, 'ello. The anorak did the trick, did it?'

Adam grinned back. 'Don't wait up,' he said nonchalantly. 'I might be quite late.' And he was gone.

Matthew picked up the leyline-map and studied it intently. Fifty-three of them, all converging on Milbury. Margaret had told him that no other place in the country claimed so many. A mind-boggling thought suddenly occurred to him: suppose this village was not merely *a* power centre, but *the* power centre…?

Adam let himself out of the cottage and began to walk through the village toward the Museum. It was so dark that he had to stop several times to get his bearings, but it wasn't until he passed the pub that he realised why. There were no lights anywhere, not even in the centre of the village, where the street-lamps lining the main road were usually shining brightly. It was still comparatively early, yet the whole village seemed to be deserted.

He tried the door of the pub, and found it locked. He walked around the back, but there was still no sign of life. Where on earth *was* everybody?

At least, the Museum was open. Margaret, looking very attractive in a smart tweed suit, was sitting at her desk, opening some letters. Adam had never been so glad to see anybody.

She looked up as he entered, and gave him a bright smile. 'Won't be a minute,' she called gaily. 'Just catching up on my correspondence.'

'No hurry.' He perched on the edge of her desk. 'Doesn't look as if we shall be going anywhere.'

She paused, in the act of opening a buff envelope. 'What do you mean?'

'The pub's shut. In fact, the whole village seems to be shut. Everyone seems to have disappeared.'

She stared at him. 'Again?'

'It's happened before?'

'About a month ago.'

'What do they do? Turn into werewolves, or something?'

'No idea. But now you know what I meant about being alone.' She opened the bottom drawer of her desk and produced a bottle and two glasses. 'Well. We'll just have to have our own private party.'

Adam inspected the bottle with approval. 'That's what I like. A woman who's prepared for all eventualities.'

She poured the drinks, handed him one, and raised her glass. 'Mud in your eye.'

'Likewise.'

They sipped their drinks in silence for a moment. Then Margaret picked up the buff envelope again. 'Mind if I finish this? It's always such a relief when it's over.'

'When what's over?'

60

'When I've read every crackpot letter.' She picked up a sheaf of letters from her wire tray. 'You wouldn't believe the number of maniacs who write to me every day, each one with his own harebrained theory. UFOs, Second Comings, Alchemy… you name it.' She pulled a letter out of the pile. 'Here's one of my favourites. "I have definite proof that Merlin built Stonehenge in Ireland and later flew it to Wiltshire. There remains no doubt that Stonehenge was originally a prototype spacecraft." '

Adam laughed. 'Powered by what?'

'Oh, that's easy. Psychic energy.'

'Now don't start all that again.' He wandered over to the glass case containing the model of the village, while Margaret tore open the buff envelope. 'Bluestones,' he said thoughtfully. 'I wonder if the rock dish is bluestone too?'

She didn't appear to hear him. 'Thank heavens for that,' she said, kissing the piece of paper she was holding. 'It's a bill.'

Adam bent over the case, staring at the miniature rocks. 'Imagine the problems of quarrying things that size with those primitive tools…'

'Flint axes? Yes, it must have been soul-destroying.'

'Not soul-*destroying*. They must have been inspired by some sort of religious fear, some visionary longing that kept them going. It must have taken months to quarry a single stone and trim it into shape.'

'Then transport it. Perhaps by sea from Wales. On rafts.'

He moved slowly back to her desk. 'There must have been a need. A sheer *need to* carry through such a project.'

'Yes.' She put the pile of letters back in her basket. 'The Archpriest must have been a mixture of Galileo and Attila the Hun. A madman with a dream.'

'Madman?' He gulped down the rest of his drink. 'No, I don't think so.'

'Then what do you think he was after?'

'Power. I think he was trying to create his own power centre. Which reminds me… Who owns Highfield House?'

'Mr Hendrick. Why?'

'Matt projected some of those leylines of yours into the Circle. They formed a triangle around Highfield House. He had some idea it was the real centre of the grid system.'

Margaret rose and walked over to the map on the wall. 'Fascinating.'

'I wonder if Hendrick knows,' said Adam, following her.

'About the leylines? I should think so. He's pretty well informed about the local phenomena.'

'How old is the house?'

'It's Elizabethan. But it was built on the site of earlier houses.'

'Then if your theory has any validity, that site would have had some significance.'

'It's possible. He's a bright boy, your Matthew.'

Adam tried to look modest. 'Can't think where he gets it from.'

She turned to face him, smiling. 'How about another drink?'

'Thanks.'

She moved back behind her desk and refilled the glasses. 'I remember the last time everyone did a vanishing act. We drank a toast to Absent Friends.'

'Who's "we"?'

'I was having dinner with Dr Lyle – he's the new doctor – and a farmer called Browning. Nice, ordinary people.'

'And what did they make of it?'

'Oh, they had no idea. I mean, they were just...' She stopped abruptly, looking blank and confused.

Adam took hold of her arm. 'They were what? Margaret? They were...'

She slumped down in her chair and stared moodily at her drink. 'They were recent arrivals too,' she said softly.

Matthew was sitting at his telescope in his pyjamas and dressing gown, staring down at the reflector plate. He had fixed the instrument according to Adam's co-ordinates, so that it would scan the Circle's potential alignment path, but so far his observations had merely confirmed what the chart had shown: there was not one single star or planet visible in the area. He slowly adjusted the focus, aiming for a sharp image. For a moment, the plate remained obstinately blank: then, gradually, dim shadows began to appear. He couldn't make out what they were at first, but as they became clearer, he saw that they were human shapes, and that they were moving slowly around in a circle.

He took his eye away from the lens for a moment: then looked again. Some of the shapes had now broken away from the Circle, and were fleeing from a blinding source of light in the centre. Those farthest away from the light had stopped, and were beginning to grow and solidify, as if they were turning into…

There was a sudden loud crash behind him. Matthew whirled around, his nerves jangling. His picture, which he had hung on the wall near the door, had fallen off its hook and was lying on the floor. He crossed slowly over to it, picked it up, and inspected it closely. Yes, there was no doubt about it: the strange vision he had seen on the reflector plate was an animated replica of the painting.

Bewildered, he hung the picture back on the wall and returned to his chair by the window. He suddenly felt very dizzy and rested his head on his arms for a moment, waiting for his mind to clear.

Something landed on the table in front of him with a muffled plop. Startled, he looked up, to find a pebble with a tattered piece of paper wrapped around it, resting by his elbow. He picked it up, stared at it uncertainly, then unwrapped the paper. It was the bicycle drawing he had left in Dai's trap. He stood up and peered out of the window into impenetrable darkness below.

'Dai?' he called softly. 'Are you there?'

No reply. He turned, wrenched open the door, and ran downstairs, into the garden.

'Dai?' he called again. 'Is it you?'

Still no reply. But wafting through the night air came a low, indefinable sound that chilled him to the marrow. He froze, trying to make out what it was and where it was coming from. He had never heard anything like it before, but a fragment of a poem he had once learned came into his mind: *'The murmur of innumerable bees.'* Could they be bees? No, the sound was too organised, its pitch rising and falling in a cadence that no insect could reproduce. Then what on earth was it?

His heart beating wildly, he ran down the path, opened the gate, and set off through the village, so engrossed in the sound that he didn't hear Dai, urgently calling his name.

He ran on and on as if hypnotised – stumbling through streets, climbing fences, swarming over walls, bulldozing his way through gardens – taking as direct a route as possible.

As he drew nearer, he suddenly realised what it was: people chanting. Not the tuneful chant of a church congregation, but more unearthly, more haunting, more primitive.

He stopped by one of the stones, and bent down to catch his breath. The sound was very close now, originating from somewhere beyond a nearby hedge. As he straightened up again, he found he was able to see over the hedge, into the garden of a large, imposing-looking house.

But it wasn't the house that attracted his attention: it was the ring of people that surrounded it. They were facing outwards, holding hands and moving slowly around in a circle, chanting as they went. Among them, Matthew recognised Mrs Crabtree, Mrs Warner, Miss Clegg, Bob, and all the children from the High Table at school…

He stared at the scene in utter amazement. It was a modern re-creation of his painting, with the strange chant as an unmusical accompaniment. What they were doing, he couldn't begin to guess: it looked like some ancient ceremony of great importance to the participants, because the rapturous expressions on their faces were terrifying in their intensity.

He heard a soft footstep on the grass behind him. He started to turn, but he was too late; someone grabbed his arms, pinioning them to his sides, and he felt himself being dragged sideways. He tried to steady himself, but his captor was too strong. The band of steel that encircled him grew tighter and tighter, pulling him further and further away from the house. Then, suddenly the vice-like grip relaxed. He stumbled, completely off balance, and he felt his hand touch stone.

Instantly, his mind erupted in a blaze of pain. A momentary, blinding flash of agony. Then, gratefully, it slid into unconsciousness…

CHAPTER SIX

LIGHT. A BLURRED KALEIDOSCOPE of colour. And sound. A radio with the battery run down. No... people. People speaking. Calling. Calling his name. What was it? Aaaa? Aaaat? Maaat? Matt.

A face swam into focus a few inches away. It was smiling. Why did people smile? It was such an idiotic thing to do: stretching their mouths sideways like that. It didn't mean anything. You could smile when you were happy, and you could smile when you were unhappy. It was all so pointless. Didn't show what you were *really* feeling. No, that would never do, would it? Against the rules.

He recognised that face. Someone he knew. Someone he liked. His father, that's who it was. Good for dad. Always there when he was wanted. There was no need for him to shout, though; that was terribly thoughtless of him. Didn't he realise how much his head hurt?

He raised his arm and gently pushed him away. That was better. Now, what was he saying? Hello? He must think of some witty reply.

'Hello yourself,' he replied wittily.

Adam was looking worried. 'What happened?' he was saying. 'Have you any idea what happened?'

Matthew slowly eased himself up into a sitting position. He was in bed, he discovered. In his own bedroom. How had he got there? He didn't remember going to bed at all. And what day was it? If only his head would stop throbbing for a moment.

'Matt, this is important. Try to remember. How did you come to be outside?'

'Outside where?'

Someone else appeared by the side of the bed: a portly, rubicund man with grey hair who also looked worried.

'This is Dr Lyle, Matt,' said Adam. 'He helped me carry you in. He needs to know what happened to you.'

Matthew searched his memory, but found it empty. 'Carried me in?' he said blankly.

The doctor bent down, produced a pencil-torch, and flashed it in Matthew's eyes. 'Watch this, will you, Matthew?' He moved the torch slowly from right to left. 'Follow it all the way.'

Matthew did as he was told, even though the process started his head throbbing again.

'That's it. Now all the way back... Good.' Lyle straightened up, put the torch back in his pocket, and turned to Adam. 'I don't think there's any permanent damage. I'll call back in the morning, just to make sure.'

'Thank you, doctor.' Adam moved to the foot of the bed. 'I don't understand what he was doing down there anyway. He should have been in bed.'

Lyle contemplated Matthew gravely for a moment. 'You still don't remember, young man?'

Matthew put his fingers to his temples, and tried to concentrate. He'd been in this room when something had landed on his desk. The pebble. The bicycle drawing. Dai.

'I heard someone calling,' he said slowly, 'so I went outside...' He stopped, his memory starting to shimmer back.

'Yes? Go on.' Adam leaned anxiously over the bed-rail.

'I heard this... chanting sound. In the distance, from the other side of the village. So I ran. And I saw these people. Standing in a circle and chanting. Then someone pulled me against one of the stones, and I felt this... this terrible pain...'

'Like an electric shock?'

'Yes.'

67

'And then?'

'I don't remember. I don't remember anything else.'

Lyle picked up a black bag, set it on the bed, and opened it. 'It's important he gets a good night's sleep,' he said, producing a bottle of pills. 'See that he takes two of these, will you?'

'Right.' Adam put the bottle in his pocket.

Lyle closed his bag and moved toward the door; then turned back, frowning.

'You've had a nasty bump on the head, Matthew. We really should try and find out how you came by it.'

Matthew shrugged. 'Sorry. I can't help.'

'Your father found you on the doorstep outside. Did you fall?'

'I told you, doctor. All I remember is touching that stone.'

'Well... not to worry. Just try and relax. And if you'll take my advice you won't go wandering about in the middle of the night again. Next time, it might be something worse than concussion.'

Adam followed him to the door. 'Thanks for your help.'

'Not at all. To tell you the truth, I'm glad of the exercise. These villagers are so damned healthy, I never get a call. I came here in semi-retirement after my heart attack, but I didn't expect to be totally ignored.'

Matthew suddenly noticed a blood-soaked handkerchief, lying on his bedside table. He picked it up and stared at it curiously. 'What's this?'

'You were wearing it when I found you,' said Adam. 'Someone had bandaged your head. But I don't understand why he didn't wait. Whoever it was, he might have been able to give us some answers.'

The two men went out. Matthew lay back on the pillows, inspecting the handkerchief. So someone had tended his wound and carried him back to the cottage. But why had they left him on the doorstep? It was all too confusing. No use puzzling over it now: thinking made his head hurt. He'd work it out in the morning. He closed his eyes and drifted off to sleep.

Next day, as Matthew was coming slowly down the stairs for breakfast, he heard voices in the sitting room: his father's and that of another man. But when he opened the door, he was surprised to find Adam alone. He was leaning out of the window, calling to somebody outside.

'Who were you talking to?'

Adam closed the window and moved back to the breakfast table. 'Some man wanted to know how you were.'

'What did he look like?'

'Like he needed a bath. Said he was a friend of yours.'

'Dai.'

'Who's Dai?'

'A poacher.'

'Providing you with illicit rabbit, is he? How's the head?'

Matthew felt the large bump on the back of his skull. 'Okay. I think.'

'Hungry?'

'Starving.'

'Yes, sounds like you're back to normal.' Adam turned and called into the kitchen. 'Mrs Crabtree.' She appeared in the doorway. 'The invalid would like some breakfast.'

She gazed at Matthew, full of motherly concern. 'Poor dear. How do you feel?'

Matthew stared back at her. It was hard to believe that this was the same woman whose ecstatic face he had picked out from the rest of the villagers the night before.

'Matt,' said Adam sharply. 'Mrs Crabtree asked you how you felt this morning.'

'All right, thanks. Bit of a headache.'

'I'm not surprised. It's hard stuff, stone.'

'What stone?'

'The doorstep. That's where you fell, wasn't it?'

'Was it?' Matthew couldn't keep the hostility out of his voice.

There was an uncomfortable silence. Mrs Crabtree wiped her hands on her apron, looking nervous.

'Well, what would you like, then? Some nice scrambled eggs?'

'Yes. Anything.'

She bustled back into the kitchen, and Matthew took his place at the table. Adam looked at him coldly.

'That wasn't very polite.'

Matthew lowered his voice. 'She was there, dad. Last night. She was part of that circle I was telling you about.'

Adam took a mouthful of toast. 'You sure you didn't dream all that?'

'You found me outside, didn't you? You didn't dream *that*.'

'You could have sleepwalked.'

'Dad, it all happened. Up to the time I blacked out, it all happened just as I said.'

'Well, I shouldn't let it upset you. What you saw was probably some traditional local ceremony. A lot of these villages have ancient rites and customs they perpetuate… even though their origins may be totally forgotten.'

Matthew leaned toward him, speaking in an urgent whisper. 'You don't understand. It wasn't just a Morris Dance or a village sing-song. The people in that circle looked as if they were… I don't know… possessed.'

Adam stopped munching for a moment. 'And where did all this take place?'

'Outside some big house. On the other side of the village.'

'Could you find it again?'

'I think so.'

There was a tap on the door, and Dr Lyle poked his head inside. 'Morning.'

'Morning, doctor,' said Adam. 'Come in.'

Lyle entered and set down his bag. 'Well? How's my one and only patient? No after-effects, I hope?'

70

Matthew grinned. 'Not so far.'

'Let's have a look at you.' The doctor crossed over to him, looked closely into his eyes, and examined his head wound. 'Not falling over or bumping into things?'

'No more than usual.'

'Hmm. Well, I should take it easy for a bit.'

'Don't worry,' said Adam. 'I'll keep him tranquillised.'

'Oh, I don't think that'll be necessary. When I was his age, I was always grateful for a few days off school.'

School! Sandra, Kevin, and Jimmo. Matthew knew he had to talk to them to find out if any of them had had a similar experience. And there were other questions – questions which couldn't wait a few days. The answers were too important.

He stood up, dashed across the room to collect his satchel from the peg by the door, and rushed out.

The two men looked at each other in amazement.

'Things seem to have changed since you were a boy,' said Adam drily.

'Incredible.' Lyle shook his head in disbelief. 'That anyone could be *that* keen…'

'Yes,' said Adam thoughtfully. 'I've never known him to miss breakfast before.'

Matthew waited for Sandra in the corridor outside the classroom. Bob passed, with a group of High Table children, wishing him 'Happy Day.' Matthew didn't reply: for some reason which he couldn't explain, he regarded everyone who had taken part in the previous night's ceremony as his enemy. And when one was surrounded by enemies, one had to choose one's friends carefully.

Sandra appeared, her dark eyes refreshingly solemn. He grabbed her arm and dragged her away down the corridor so they couldn't be overheard.

'Ow,' she said. 'You're hurting my arm.'

'Sorry, but I want to ask you something. You remember when we first met? You said new people in the village had to stick together?'

'Yes.'

'What did you mean?'

'I meant it was safer.'

'Why?'

She stared down the corridor toward the classroom. 'We have to protect ourselves.'

'Protect ourselves? From what?'

'I don't know really. It's just something I feel.'

Matthew thought for a moment. 'And my first day at school. You told Kevin I *must* be human, because I'd only just arrived.'

'That's right.'

'So after people have been here a while, they aren't human any more? Like most of those kids in there?'

The dark eyes clouded. 'Yes,' she said slowly. 'Something seems to happen to them. I don't know what it is, but something seems to happen.'

'They change?'

'You must have noticed. Some of us are normal, and the rest are… Happy Ones.'

'They don't look very happy to me.'

'I know. They never lose their tempers, always do as they're told. But they're like…' She hesitated, searching for the word.

'Zombies?' suggested Matthew.

'Yes. Zombies. Robots. Puppets.' She looked around, saw that they were alone, and began to look uneasy. 'We'd better go in…'

She tried to move past him, but he barred her way. 'There's a man called Dai.'

'The poacher?'

'Yes. You know him?'

'Sort of. I think he's potty. Always trying to warn me… telling me to be careful.'

'He told me if I ever needed sanctuary, I should go to him for help.'

'No, no.' She shook her head emphatically. 'If we ever need *help*, we should go to the *Sanctuary*.'

'Where's that?'

'Linnet Barrow. Dai lives there.'

'How far is it?'

'Not far. At the end of the Avenue.'

Matthew tried to remember exactly what the old man had said about where he went. Never beyond the sight of the stones. Never out of their grasp. A strange choice of words...

'So he *does* live outside the Circle,' he said, trying to make sense of it all.

'Yes.' Sandra seemed to read his thought. 'But still within the stones...'

She turned and hurried off down the corridor. Matthew followed her into the classroom.

Adam stood staring out of the cottage window, while Mrs Crabtree cleared away the breakfast things. The question was – had Matthew received his bump on the head *after* seeing the chanting circle of villagers, or *before*? If the latter, then the whole business could be dismissed as hallucination. But even that didn't explain what he was doing on the doorstep in his pyjamas and dressing gown, with a dirty handkerchief tied around his head.

Matthew's poacher friend – what was his name? Dai? – had seemed to know something about the affair. Perhaps it was he who had bound his wound; the handkerchief was so dirty, it could well have come from a pocket of that scruffy coat. But then, why hadn't he waited? And why had he dashed off so quickly after making sure the patient was all right? Could he have had something to hide?

Matthew had said Mrs Crabtree had been part of the circle. Well, there was a very easy way to find out whether his story was fact or fiction.

'Mrs Crabtree,' he said, turning toward her. 'Forgive the impertinence, but... do you mind telling me what you were doing last night?'

'Doing, sir?' She looked flustered. 'You mean... before I went to bed?'

'That's right.'

'Why, I was over at Mr Hendrick's house. He had one of his little get-togethers.'

'Did you sing? Dance?'

'Oh yes, sir. You can't have a proper celebration without singing and dancing, now can you?'

So that was it: an innocent country dance, which Matthew had mistaken for some kind of sinister ritual. Probably influenced by that blasted picture of his. It looked so like Milbury, that an ordinary village ceremony might well assume a nightmarish aspect in the mind of an impressionable boy.

Adam wondered what Margaret would make of the picture, and how it compared with the various charts in the Museum. He decided to drop in with it on his way out to the Circle; it would be interesting to get an archaeologist's opinion.

He went up to Matthew's bedroom, took the picture off the wall, and returned just as Mrs Crabtree was disappearing into the kitchen with the breakfast tray.

'Oh, by the way, Mrs C,' he said, picking up his magnetometer. 'What happens about telegrams? Does one have to collect them from the Post Office?'

'No need for that, sir. Mrs Warner delivers them personally.'

'I see.'

'You're expecting one, then? Today?'

'Yes. If it comes while I'm out, sign for it, would you?'

'Of course, sir.'

Adam strapped the aluminum magnetometer-case over his shoulder and, carrying the picture under his arm, set off for the Museum. It was a glorious day, and the village basked sleepily in the midsummer sun. No, this place was a dream, not a nightmare: as far removed from the horror of the picture as the Hallelujah Chorus was from a funeral dirge.

Nevertheless, Margaret was taken aback when he showed her the painting. 'Extraordinary,' she said, studying it intently. 'Quite extraordinary.'

'Could it be Milbury?' asked Adam. 'As a primitive settlement?'

'It's certainly possible.' She carried the picture over to the display model of the Circle as it was in Neolithic times. 'Yes, there's an uncanny resemblance. The stones are in the same positions. And there's the hill...' She propped the painting up on the glass case and stepped back, comparing it with the model. 'There are fewer stones in the picture, of course. It looks like the Circle as it is today. There's the Avenue leading to the Sanctuary, the head of the Solar Serpent. I'd say it was definitely Milbury.'

Adam moved to stand by her side. 'So,' he said thoughtfully, 'if the subject's real, it's likely that the story it tells has some real significance? A brilliant source of light that seems to have the power to turn people to stone. A man and a boy escaping toward the Sanctuary. Fear and terror... ancient and primordial... But what does it all mean?'

Margaret shivered. 'Some pagan superstition, perhaps? Beginning as a ritual, and ending with all the worshippers being... transformed. Terrifying.' She moved away. 'We're lucky to be living in this century.'

'Is it so different?' Adam looked around at the various maps and charts pinned to the walls. 'There's still a lot going on we don't understand.'

She sat down at her desk. 'You mean, like a whole village that suddenly disappears?'

'Oh, I've solved that mystery. They were over at Hendrick's house. He had some sort of party.'

'To which everyone was invited but us?'

'Perhaps we haven't been here long enough. According to Matthew, they were doing some sort of circular dance. Sounded pretty complicated.'

Margaret stared at him. 'He saw them?'

'Yes.' He told her about Matthew's nocturnal adventure, of his puzzling accident, and of the anonymous benefactor who had bandaged his head.

She listened with growing concern. 'And how is he this morning?'

'Right as rain. I tried to persuade him to take the day off, but he wasn't having any. Insisted on going to school.'

'Not like Sandra. She'd have stayed away for weeks.'

'She finds it tough going?'

'Very.'

'So does Matt. Even the maths, which is odd. He's never had any difficulty before.'

Margaret picked up a pencil and started doodling on her notepad. 'A ring of people holding hands, eh? I didn't know they did that here.'

'Did what?'

'It's known as clipping the church. The parishioners clasp hands and move around it in a clockwise direction – with the sun – then advance and retreat three times. It's an old custom: something to do with renewing one's faith by binding bodies and souls together.'

Adam frowned. 'But they were nowhere near the church.'

'I know. It just doesn't make sense. Unless…'

'Unless what?'

'Unless Hendrick's house is the next best thing. The church is deconsecrated. It's in the gift of the manor, and hasn't had an incumbent for years.'

'Why not?'

'Milbury's too small, I suppose. A congregation of fifty-odd souls wouldn't be an economic proposition.'

Adam looked at his watch. 'Well, I must do some work. How about shutting up shop for an hour or two and coming out to the Circle with me?'

She brightened. 'I'd enjoy that. Doesn't look as if I'm going to get any customers this morning, and if anyone asks, I can always say I'm widening my knowledge.'

She locked up the Museum, and they walked out to the nearest stone. Adam unpacked his magnetometer, explaining how it worked.

'It's really very simple,' he said. 'This instrument consists of a short magnet, with a long, non-magnetic pointer at right angles across it, pivoted at the junction. The pointer swings along a circular scale, thus enabling deflections of the short magnet to be measured.'

Margaret frowned. 'Thanks,' she said drily. 'That's clear as mud.'

He grinned. 'Sorry. Just showing off.' He handed her a notebook and pencil. 'Mind copying down the reading? Just watch the pointer.'

He switched on the machine, and the needle jumped around the dial. She waited a moment to make sure it was steady, then wrote down the degree of variation.

'There you are,' she said, holding out the notebook.

But Adam took no notice. He was staring at the dial with a puzzled expression on his face. 'Incredible,' he said softly.

'Incredibly good? Or incredibly bad?'

'Hang on a minute.' He moved the instrument to the other side of the rock. The needle remained stationary.

'Well?' Margaret was becoming impatient. 'What does it mean?'

He turned to face her. 'What do you know about magnetic fields?'

'Teach me, Professor. I know the earth has one.'

'So do rocks. You've heard of lodestones – primitive compasses?'

'Yes.'

'Well, normally rocks should align with the direction of the earth's magnetic field at the time that the rock stratum was formed.'

'And this doesn't?'

'No. It aligns with the *present* magnetic field.'

'Which means?'

Adam didn't reply. Seeing something lying in the grass a few yards away, he walked over and picked it up. It was a rusty horseshoe. 'Watch,' he said, and threw the horseshoe at the rock.

There was a loud clang as the iron hit the stone, but the horseshoe, instead of falling back to the ground, stuck to the rock like a limpet.

Margaret stared at it incredulously. 'Stone acting like a magnet? It's not possible.'

'There's only one explanation,' said Adam quietly. 'Some tremendous energy has passed through that rock. And very recently…'

CHAPTER SEVEN

'THE REASON I'VE KEPT you in,' Miss Clegg was saying, 'has nothing to do with punishment. Rome wasn't built in a day, and I expect it will be some time before you are able to take your places at the High Table. But I have reason to think that one of you – I shan't tell you which one – is on the verge of making a breakthrough. If I'm right, I want his or her success to be an inspiration to the rest: an example of what each of you will eventually be able to achieve…'

Matthew and Sandra glanced at each other. They, together with Kevin and Jimmo, had been asked to stay behind after class, and Matthew had feared the worst. But Miss Clegg seemed in a good mood, and she didn't appear to be setting them any extra work. She just wanted to give them a pep talk.

But which one of them was she talking about? Matthew knew it wasn't him; his head still ached and he'd never felt less like being on the verge of a breakthrough. Sandra looked as bewildered as he was. And as for Kevin and Jimmo – the thought of either of them ever sitting at the High Table was laughable. Neither of them could even add.

Miss Clegg moved to the blackboard. On it were some incomprehensible problems she had set the bright children. 'Now,' she said, 'I know that questions like these have so far been beyond you. But I wonder if today anyone feels like attempting one of them?'

Sandra groaned. Kevin blew a soft raspberry. Nothing had changed. Matthew leaned back in his chair, knowing that Miss Clegg was wasting her time. If none of them could solve the problems yesterday, why should they do any better today? They weren't suddenly going to change into geniuses overnight.

Or were they? Out of the corner of his eye, Matthew saw Jimmo slowly raise his hand. Was he out of his tiny mind? He'd have difficulty in counting his father's cows.

Miss Clegg was smiling at him. 'Yes, Jimmo?'

'I think I could do them, miss.'

'Splendid.' She held out the chalk. 'Suppose you work out that first Bessel transform?'

Jimmo stood up, took the chalk, and began to write on the blackboard. Slowly at first, then with increasing speed as he gained confidence, the complicated equation resolved itself.

Matthew stared, open-mouthed. It was a miracle – there was no other word for it. So it *was* possible to turn into a genius overnight. He looked at the others, and saw that they were equally bewildered. Kevin seemed to have completely run out of raspberries.

His work done, Jimmo handed the chalk back to Miss Clegg, smiling a vacant, happy smile. She put her arm around his shoulders.

'Bravo, Jimmo. Tomorrow, you may take your place at the High Table.' She turned to the others. 'You see what can be done? Sooner or later, you'll all be able to achieve that standard, I promise you. So don't give up hope. It's just a question of time.' Pushing Jimmo in front of her, she walked out of the classroom.

Kevin rose and crossed slowly over to the blackboard, shaking his head in awe. 'I don't get it,' he said. 'Yesterday a dumdum, and today, he's doing tricks like that. What happened in between?'

'Same thing that happened to the rest of them,' said Sandra softly.

'And what's that?'

'I don't know. But whatever it is, I don't want it to happen to me.'

Kevin pointed at Matthew. 'What about bright boy here? If *he* gets the treatment, he'll make Einstein look like a beginner.'

'Treatment?' said Matthew. 'You think that's what Jimmo got? Some kind of treatment?'

'Don't ask.' Kevin picked up the eraser, and savagely wiped the blackboard clean.

'Well, if it *is* a treatment,' Matthew went on, 'who gives it? And why?'

'We'll just have to wait and see, won't we?'

'What do you mean?'

Kevin shrugged. 'Obvious. There's only us three left. It's just a question of who's next.'

There was an uneasy silence. The prospect of being turned into a Happy One hung over each of them like a pall. But where did the threat come from? If they didn't know that, how could they protect themselves against it?

'We must try and stick together,' said Matthew urgently. 'Compare notes whenever we can. Then no one can take us by surprise…'

There was a soft tap on the window. Matthew jumped up, his heart racing, to see Dai's face flattened against the heavy casement.

'Dai.' Relieved that the visitor was someone he recognised, he ran over and opened the catch.

Dai peered suspiciously into the room to make sure the coast was clear. 'Sorry, boy,' he rumbled. 'It had to be done, see?'

'What had to be done?'

'Had to get you away from there. Shock treatment – that was the only way. Dangerous, it was.' He heaved himself through the narrow opening, puffing and blowing with the effort. Once inside, he collapsed onto the window seat, exhausted.

'So it was you?' said Matthew accusingly. 'It was you who grabbed my arm last night?'

Dai nodded, panting for breath. 'Your saviour, I am. Thank your lucky stars I was there to save you.'

'Save me? From what?'

'The past. Aye, that's it. The past. My past. And your future.'

'I don't understand.'

'I'll let you into a secret, boy. Neither do I.'

Sandra moved to join them. 'Dai, you do understand. You understand *something*. Which is more than we do.'

The old man contemplated her in silence for a moment.

'I *feel* things, miss. That's not the same as understanding.'

'What do you feel?' asked Kevin, sitting next to him on the seat.

'What do I feel? I feel haunted.' The children looked at each other in alarm. 'No, not by ghosts, or anything like that.' He turned and gazed out of the window toward the village. 'But something happened here a long time ago. And it's happening again today.'

'Bogey, bogey,' said Kevin, trying to lighten the mood of foreboding that Dai had created. 'Any idea what?'

'Everyone turned to stone,' said Matthew suddenly.

The others stared at him. 'Go on, boy,' said Dai. 'Explain yourself.'

'I have a picture at home, I think it's meant to be Milbury in the old days. And it shows people turning into stone.'

Sandra shuddered. 'You mean, all those stones out there might be *people?*'

Kevin giggled nervously. 'What a petrifying thought.'

But Matthew didn't laugh. He was trying to think back – to remember the impression the picture had first made on him. 'No, I think it's more complicated than that. I think this village is... oh, I can't explain.'

'Like a maze, it is,' said Dai half to himself, 'with treasure at the centre. Trouble is, there's danger too.'

'What kind of danger?' asked Kevin.

'If I knew that, we could avoid it, couldn't we? But we can't.'

'Why not?'

'Because it's there. In the past. And the future.'

Matthew wished the old man wouldn't keep talking in riddles. 'You say there's treasure here,' he said. 'What treasure?'

'The most priceless treasure of all. Knowledge.' He fumbled in the pocket of his coat, and produced a thick round disc. 'What do you make of this?' he asked, holding it up to the light.

'What is it? Where did you get it?' Matthew held out his hand for the disc, but Dai clutched it to his body protectively.

'Part of the treasure,' said Dai mysteriously. 'I found it. It came to me. Interest your father, maybe?'

'Dad?' Matthew glanced at Sandra. 'More in your mum's line, isn't it?'

'Yes. Shall I show it to her?'

'No.' Dai shrank away from her. 'It's mine. It came to me.'

Matthew crouched down beside him. 'We won't take it, then. We'll make a tracing. Will you let us do that?'

'Like a brass-rubbing!' said Kevin excitedly. 'I'll get some tracing paper.' He ran over to his desk.

Dai closed his eyes, still hugging the disc. 'It's a key,' he said softly. 'That's what it is. My key...'

But he let them make a tracing, and the children cycled over to the Museum to show it to Margaret.

She studied the design with interest.

'The original's made of clay, you think?'

'Either that or some kind of stone,' said Sandra. 'It looked very old.'

Margaret pinned the tracing to the wall and inspected it closely. 'Interesting,' she said thoughtfully.

'Looks like a snake,' said Matthew.

'No. I think it's a serpent.'

'What's the difference?' asked Kevin. 'They both give me the willies.'

'A serpent's bigger and more powerful. It's also a symbol.'

'A symbol of what?'

'It was the original guardian of knowledge. Later, serpents were supposed to protect sacred hills and mazes.'

'Dai knew that,' said Matthew. 'He said something about the village being like a maze, with treasure at the centre.'

'And the treasure was knowledge,' Sandra added.

Margaret frowned. 'How did he know that?'

'He didn't *know*, mum. He just felt it.'

Kevin peered at the tracing. 'And the danger in the maze may have been this yukky snake-thing.'

'Of course!' Margaret suddenly remembered where she had seen the design before. 'Dai's feelings are remarkably accurate. This symbol has a special significance here.'

'The church!' said Sandra suddenly. 'There's a serpent carved on the font.' She giggled. 'It's biting the foot of a bishop.'

Margaret smiled. 'That's right. And I told you what that meant, remember?'

'It represents the battle between pagan and Christian.'

'Exactly. After the battle was over, Christians often built their churches on the sites of the pagan temples – ground that was already sacred. But they couldn't be sure the ancient religion had been completely stamped out, so the carving on the font was probably intended as a warning.'

Matthew felt a prickling sensation at the nape of his neck. 'A warning?'

'To be constantly on their guard.'

'Against the power of the serpent?'

'Yes.'

Sandra thought for a moment. 'Then this thing of Dai's – whatever it is – is pagan?'

'Oh, there's no doubt about that. Some sort of charm or amulet to keep the owner from harm, perhaps. I'd love to see the original.'

Matthew looked at the others. 'We'll get it,' he said firmly, 'even if we have to bring the owner.'

That evening, when Adam arrived at the pub, he found Hendrick at the bar. 'Hello,' he said cheerfully. 'I've been waiting for you.'

'Me? Why?'

'First things first. What'll you have?'

'No, I'll get them.' He pointed at Hendrick's glass. 'Two of those, please, George.'

As the landlord moved away to fetch the drinks, Hendrick delved into his pocket and produced a yellow envelope. 'Mrs Crabtree told me there was a telegram for you. I promised to deliver it.'

'Ah, thanks. I've been waiting for that.' Adam tore open the envelope and read the message carefully.

Hendrick sipped his drink, watching him. 'Not bad news, I hope?'

'No. It's from Mount Palomar Observatory. In answer to a telegram of my own.'

'Oh?'

'Just some research they've done for me.'

'Concerning Milbury?'

'Yes. I wondered if the stones were aligned to a point immediately *above* the Circle… and if so, what was on the alignment path. I could find no connection between the Circle and any of the major stars or planets. It just didn't make sense.'

Hendrick's dark eyes regarded him with interest. 'And now it does?'

'In a way.' Adam waved the telegram. 'According to this, it's aligned to a supernova that exploded centuries before Christ – somewhere around the start of man's rational existence. There's nothing there now but a black hole: a huge mass of imploding energy…'

'*I* could have told you that,' said Hendrick quietly.

'You?' The landlord brought the drinks, and Adam paid for them. 'What do you know about the supernova?'

Hendrick smiled. 'Let's go and sit down.'

They moved over to one of the tables. 'It's unfair of me,' Hendrick went on. 'I should have introduced myself properly when we first met.'

Adam stared at him, the penny finally dropping. 'Of course. Hendrick's Supernova. You're Raphael Hendrick, the astronomer.'

'Ex-astronomer. I resigned my chair at Cambridge five years ago.'

'I remember. I always wondered why.'

'Because of some papers.'

'Papers?'

Hendrick toyed with his glass. 'They were unearthed by a colleague. Written in dog-Latin, in a style earlier than Bede's… about sixth century. A mish-mash of fact and fiction about Megalithic Britain – legends and stories handed down through the centuries, which the author had assembled in some sort of order. None of them could be authenticated, of course, but there was one event which, because of my discovery of the supernova, made me sit up and take notice.'

'What was that?' asked Adam, fascinated.

'Someone in this village – Weal Wicca, as it was then called – was reported by bardic tradition as having seen a star explode.'

'So that's why you settled in Milbury? Because someone here actually witnessed the beginning of the black hole?'

'It was like coming home.'

'Even though there's nothing there?'

Hendrick glanced up at him sharply. 'The black hole's there.'

'I meant, of course, there's nothing to see.'

'But that's what's so intriguing, don't you think? To know it's there, and yet not be able to see it?'

Adam grinned. 'I'm afraid my interests are more earthbound.'

'You know which constellation it's in?'

'Ursa Major.'

'Exactly. The Great Bear. And as you also probably know, the bear was once an object of veneration. The Bear Cult is one of the earliest known religions.'

'Originated, perhaps, by that primitive cave-dweller who saw your supernova explode?'

For some reason, this seemed to offend Hendrick. 'Primitive cave-dweller?' he said coolly. 'According to legend, he was a visionary. A spiritual leader. A man of destiny.'

'I beg his pardon,' said Adam soothingly.

'I think you might be well advised to do so.'

There was no doubt that, as far as Hendrick was concerned, the conversation had taken an unfortunate turn. Adam was at a loss: what had he said to cause this sudden iciness? It was time to change the subject.

'By the way,' he said, 'my son tells me he saw some sort of dance taking place outside your house last night.'

Hendrick looked surprised. 'He must have been up very late.'

'I thought he'd invented it at first. But Mrs Crabtree tells me it's not unusual.'

'No, no. It's an old custom. My house is supposed to have been built on sacred ground, you see, and the villagers form a ring to protect it from... well... evil.'

Adam thought for a moment. 'Sacred ground, eh? Could that have anything to do with the leylines?'

'Leylines?'

'According to Matthew, Highfield House is completely surrounded by them. I wondered if the ground was sacred because they formed a sort of protective barrier.'

Hendrick stared at him, impressed. 'You mean, like the ring of villagers?'

'Yes.'

'Interesting theory. Well, you must come to dinner soon, and put it to the test. See if you feel any... vibrations.'

'Thanks. I'd like that.'

'Can't ask you yet, I'm afraid, because of protocol. One has to be careful in a place this size. If I didn't invite everyone in strict rotation, I'd get into terrible trouble.'

'I understand. But I'd be interested to see one of those village rituals. Next time there is one, would you let me know?'

Hendrick finished off his drink. 'There's one tomorrow, as a matter of fact. Not at my house... near the stones. It's Wiccastane – the day the people used to bury one of them. Nowadays, we have a Morris Dance instead.'

'A Morris Dance?' Adam winced. 'I'm afraid they rather bore me. They all look the same.'

'I know what you mean. Nevertheless, the villagers enjoy them. And to tell you the truth, Wiccastane's only an excuse. They dance whenever they feel like it, on any day of the year. There's always some old festival they can use as a precedent.'

'Well, I can't promise to come. I'm way behind schedule, and I've a lot of work to do.'

Hendrick contemplated him in silence for a moment. 'Try to be there. For complete fulfillment, one should play one's full part in the community. And I'm sure you'll come to appreciate our little ceremonies. Everyone does.'

There was no doubt in his voice. It was a statement of fact.

The following day – a Saturday – Adam and Matthew called for Margaret and Sandra at the Museum. Kevin and his father, Dr Lyle, were also there, and the six of them set off through the empty streets, guided by the sound of music. In the distance, a fiddle was playing a stately jig, accompanied by the rhythmic jingle of bells.

As they came into the open, Matthew saw that the whole village seemed to have turned out. In a far corner, near the edge of the Circle, a large group of onlookers was watching the Morris Dancers weaving in and out of each other, the bells on their feet jingling in unison. The fiddler was George, the landlord of the pub.

They strolled across the grass to join the spectators. The doctor asked Margaret about the origins of Morris Dancing, and why the participants had bells strapped to their ankles.

'The bells are to help them keep together,' she said, 'but as for the origins... well, we can only guess. It's certainly very old, and I believe it was supposed to help fertilise the crops in the spring.'

The rhythm was very infectious. As the dancers formed and reformed themselves into intricate patterns, Matthew and Sandra started to clap in time to the music. The villagers nodded encouragement, and soon everyone was clapping. It was a gay, merry scene, and Matthew began to wonder why he had felt so jittery ever since coming to Milbury. It all looked so *right:* a small, peaceful community perpetuating an ancient custom of their ancestors. There was nothing at all to worry about.

Two strange-looking figures began to weave in and out of the dancers. One, much larger than the other, wore a horse's head made of pasteboard, and a wickerwork frame around its waist to represent the body. The smaller of the two wore the white mask of a clown, and was beating those around him with an inflated bladder tied to a stick.

Matthew turned to Margaret. 'Who are they?'

'One's the hobby-horse,' she told him, 'and the other's the fool. They're both traditional figures but don't ask me why. I think the fool's there to spur people on to greater effort.'

Gradually, almost without Matthew noticing it, the shape of the dance became circular, with the two masked figures in the centre. Then the music suddenly stopped, and the dancers remained motionless, waiting expectantly. In the ensuing silence, the figures took off their masks…

Margaret gasped.

Adam glanced at her. 'What's the matter?'

'That man. The one with the horse's mask. It's Tom Browning.'

'And the other one's Jimmo,' said Matthew quietly. 'They're not by any chance father and son?'

Margaret stared at them grimly. 'That's right.'

'So?' said Adam. 'What's the mystery?'

'Tom's a farmer. The one the doctor and I were having dinner with, that first night when everyone disappeared. He's one of the newcomers.'

'I still don't see why you're so upset.'

Margaret looked up at Lyle. 'Tell him, doctor.'

'It's out of character,' said Lyle, frowning. 'Browning was so contemptuous of these local superstitions. Said they were a waste of time… anachronisms. Yet there he is, right in the thick of it.'

Adam looked at the two figures in the centre of the Circle. They were staring up into the sky, as if waiting for a signal. 'Well, he's obviously changed his mind. Nothing wrong with that, is there?'

Suddenly, Jimmo jumped onto his father's back. The two of them raised their arms to the heavens and cried out in unison: 'Happy Day. Happy Day. Happy Day…'

Adam felt a sudden chill. For standing on the other side of the Circle, towering over the rest of the spectators, was Hendrick. And he was smiling. And behind the smile, there was a hint of triumph.

CHAPTER EIGHT

BACK AT THE COTTAGE, Lyle stared out into the street, trying to spot the flaws in Margaret's line of crazy reasoning. Adam went straight into the kitchen to order tea from Mrs Crabtree, and it was Sandra who broke the silence in her usual no-nonsense way.

'And then there were six…? Is Mum right? Or are we imagining it all?'

'My imagination's not that good,' protested Margaret quietly.

'It's certainly weird, that Jimmo bit…' Kevin surfaced from among the chesterfield cushions, legs everywhere. 'I mean, he was never exactly anything more than a promising wing-half – so what turned him into Mastermind overnight?'

'Whatever it was has got me jumpy and I don't mind admitting it,' said Lyle, without turning around. 'I suppose I should have been more aware of these changes than any of us here but somehow I've not noticed a thing until this afternoon, until Margaret's theorizing started things clicking in my mind.'

'You've only just arrived yourself,' said Adam as he closed the kitchen door behind him carefully. 'You've not had the comparisons in behaviour to work from and besides, for all their friendliness, people in Milbury are as close as any when it comes to letting others in on their privacy. Try it. Knock on any door. You'll get a big smile and a "Happy Day" but you'll never get past the *Welcome* on the mat.'

Matthew had caught his father's glance as he closed the kitchen door and realised that the act was not without thought.

91

Once or twice Matthew had fancied that deaf-as-a-post Mrs Happyday Crabtree heard rather more than she pretended. Coupled with his initial dislike and the fact that she had been part of the circle around Hendrick's house, his father's growing caution caused him no surprise at all.

Lyle pulled a chair toward the table. 'Let's keep things in perspective. It's not as if we were being killed off one by one. What are we frightened of? What *is* this disease we're so afraid of catching?'

Adam was firm. 'Happy Day-itis.'

'Exactly,' snorted the doctor. 'So we say "Happy Day" to each other instead of "Good morning." What's so terrible about that?'

'You're talking about a symptom, doctor,' said Margaret. 'The disease goes much deeper.'

Adam nodded. 'It's an epidemic and there doesn't seem to be an antidote...'

The doctor tilted his chair back and stared from one to the other, challengingly. 'An antidote to being happy?' He wanted to spark the possible truth with his questions...

Margaret said hastily, 'I suggested that... well, we do seem to be very much out of step here, don't we? And not merely because we are newcomers...' Her voice trailed away unhappily.

Adam nodded and reached across to touch her hand. Matthew watched his concern for her with a curious feeling of detachment, as though he had known for a long time his father's need to care for someone other than himself.

'So why don't we keep all our sensors alert,' said Kevin, flicking idly through an old copy of an American astrophysics magazine. 'That way, we can amass relevant data and compute possible think parameters.' He turned the magazine the right way up but the stargraphs still made no sense to him.

Lyle nodded. 'He's fond of jargon, my son, but he's right now and again. There's no doubt that as outsiders we may become, what shall I say... targets...?'

'Victims,' said Adam grimly. The word itself as much as the tone with which it was delivered caused an awkwardness among them.

Sandra refused to be shaken from her role of debate umpire. 'What say you, silent and deep?'

Matthew was saved the difficulty of reply by the clink of crockery from the kitchen and the rattle of the door handle. 'I think we should concentrate on Mrs C's cucumber sandwiches for the next few minutes.'

'And my chocolate cake… I don't want none of it left,' said Mrs Crabtree as she pottered in with the huge tray and started scattering cutlery and plates of goodies about the table.

Matthew glanced at his father. Had she heard his last remark? Adam was fully occupied pouring lemonade for Sandra and Kevin, but as he turned to hand a glass full of ice and foaming lemon to his son, he said quietly, 'Thanks for the warning.'

The talk became general until the housekeeper bustled back into the kitchen, then Matthew muttered to Sandra, 'She gives me the creeps.'

'Me too,' she agreed.

'She gives me chocolate cake,' said Kevin, eyeing it hungrily over the edge of a fast-disappearing sandwich.

Lyle took up the old refrain. 'What in fact do we know for sure?' He looked around the table but nobody seemed to want to start the ball rolling again.

Matthew launched himself into the gap. 'Nothing is what we *know*… apart from the fact that families seem to change together. I mean, Jimmo and his father; whatever happened, happened to them at the same time…'

The silence developed.

Adam coughed. 'It's almost as if…' He shrugged the thought away but Margaret prompted him to continue. He smiled and said, 'No. It's too ridiculous…'

She took up his theme. 'As if it were all planned…?'

They all tried to avoid each other's eyes but Lyle stuck to his probing, questioning scepticism. 'Planned. No proof, just emotional reaction to unspecified data… Planned by whom?'

Matthew blurted out, 'Or by *what?*'

Adam whistled softly and looked around the puzzled, subdued group of friends. 'That is a can of beans…'

Margaret nodded. 'And until it's fully opened, I suggest we keep in close touch. As Kevin has suggested, go around with our eyes open and pool our information.'

The suggestion was met with the total silence of acceptance.

Margaret went on, 'But don't let's forget that we're not the only outsiders in the village. There's Dai… perhaps it would be a good idea if we had another try at getting hold of that disc of his?'

'And what about Hendrick?' said the doctor as he shrugged himself into his coat. 'He's another who seems unaffected by the phenomenon. Matter of fact, he's invited Kevin and me to dinner this evening.'

Matthew thought for a moment. 'I know why Dai's immune. Because he lives at the Sanctuary. He says he's safe there.'

'And Hendrick's house is at the centre of the leyline grid,' said Margaret. 'Perhaps they give him the same sort of protection.'

Adam turned to Lyle. 'If you've been summoned to the presence, doctor, you'll be able to do a little detective work.'

'Afraid not. I had to turn him down.'

Adam looked surprised.

'Pity,' said the doctor, 'I want to take a look over that house but tonight I'm off to Melsham to see an old patient of mine. She doesn't trust her new doctor and wants me to give her a check-up. So instead of dinner at Highfield House, I have a thirty-mile drive ahead of me.'

Adam suggested that next time Lyle was invited to Hendrick's house, he shouldn't let anything, not even a patient, stand in his way.

'We need all the information we can get,' murmured Margaret.

The doctor agreed. Actually, he seemed rather pleased at the chance to get out of the village. He explained, 'It's the fact that somebody needs me. Apart from Matthew's knock on the head, I've had practically nothing to exercise me since I came… This village is too healthy for my liking.'

Moments after they had gone, Matthew saw Lyle's gloves on the back of the wing chair. He grabbed them and started for the door. A searing pain shot through his body and his hand felt the gloves writhe and move of their own volition. The pain became a sound, more beautiful than anything he had ever heard, not music, but pure sound. The sound became light and through the sweet aching brilliance came the figures of the doctor, Margaret, Sandra, and Kevin . . walking, talking past the church, toward the Museum… Some part of Matthew's mind struggled against the impossibility of the vision and almost against his will the figures faded, leaving an emptiness and a sense of loss which he had never felt before. The gloves leaped from his hand and fell on the table.

Matthew stared down at them. He stretched out his hand tentatively and touched the worn black leather. His hand began to shake, uncontrollably. The pain began again…

Adam's voice came through the pain, quiet and conversational. The gloves became gloves, Matthew felt absolute reality return, again with that feeling of void and regret, as though he had experienced a greater reality… His mind reeled.

'Are those Lyle's? Drop them in to him on the way to school tomorrow, would you?'

Matthew waited, giving himself time to recover. 'Dad, they feel funny… full of… static…'

Adam looked up, surprised. Matthew forestalled the obvious...

'I know, first principles, leather's a non-conductor. But it's there...'

Adam picked up the gloves and examined them carefully. A pair of comfortable old black leather gloves that had given good service, would become driving gloves in time, and end their life on a hook in a potting shed. He grinned at his son who stared at the gloves, discomfited. 'I think that bang on the head is finally getting through to you.' He tossed the gloves to Matthew, who let them fall on the table. One fell with the wrist opening gaping toward him, and despite himself Matthew felt compelled to slip his hand inside the warm lined interior and wriggle his fingers into a comfortable fit.

Instantly his fist spasmed shut and shot up, clenched in front of his face. He felt physically stretched, mentally winded as the old remembered pain seared into his other-conscious...

Adam spun as he heard the breath go from Matthew's body.

Matthew gasped for air, drowning in his vision. Again a wave of pain-sound, turning to light. 'I can see... I can see.'

Adam tried not to panic at the tone of his son's voice, the tight flatness of his shallow breathing, and the unflickering stare of his eyes...

The boy knew that it was important in some way that he should make his father understand, that all this was happening for some good reason... but that was in another time or place... at this moment all that was real was the vision of Dr Lyle getting into his car and driving out of the village.

'He's pleased... pleased to be leaving... I'm inside his head... I'm part of his mind...'

The car gathered pace as it approached the Avenue at the edge of the Circle. The stones sped past; the great earthwork drew closer; the gap where the road passed through, flanked by the two great sentinel sarsens at the beginning of the Avenue, approached fast. Matthew felt Lyle panic. The road was gone.

The light was black now, the sound a groan, the pain a wound across the mind…

'Something's blocking the way…' Matthew's voice faded. 'I'm tired… it's gone…'

Matthew surfaced slowly in his father's arms. Adam stared down into the white hurt of his son's experience and asked fiercely, 'Was all that for real? Did you see all that happen?'

Matthew was slow, like coming from sleep.

Adam insisted. 'You saw that?'

Matthew smiled wanly, then closed his eyes, aching for rest. 'I saw it…'

Margaret placed the tracing of the clay disc on the glass top of the display cabinet, immediately over the mounted remains of the disc found beside the barber-surgeon's body. She moved the paper about until the solar-serpent designs almost coincided…

Adam finished his tale.

'Psychometry,' said Margaret thoughtfully. 'The ability to tune in to the vibrations of inanimate objects. To receive feelings, ideas and images from them.'

'You know about it? It's nothing new?' Adam sounded as worried as before.

Margaret smiled at his confusion. Gently she explained, 'His psychic awareness is probably developing along with his sensitivity. It's not uncommon for people of Matthew's age to discover some sort of paranormal power.'

'So it's not simply an hallucination?' Adam shook his head. 'That's almost more frightening.'

'Worrying, certainly.' Margaret thought for a moment, then took down a book from a shelf. She consulted the index and flipped through the pages to the chapter she was looking for. Adam watched her riffling through the book.

'A psychometric bible?' He smiled.

'Something like that.' Margaret handed him the opened book to read for himself. 'Anna MacArthy is an eminent woman in her own field. Not an apparent nutter, but when these people start dabbling on the fringes of psychic phenomena they seem to lose much of their objectivity. She was in here only a week or two ago, a nice old biddy until she started on about the Circle and her communications with the ancients who built it.'

Adam read on. Turning a page, he glanced at a photograph of Miss MacArthy, eyes staring into the future, touching a burial urn with her fingertips and ecstatically contemplating the past. He snapped the book shut. 'Now I am worried,' he said. 'Matt has always been so… sensible. Where did this lunatic ability come from – and *why*? He simply picked up a pair of gloves and freaked out. I know he's imaginative but he's never pulled a stunt like that before.'

'Tests have been carried out under controlled conditions and while the results are confused and open to more than one interpretation, stunt is not the word I would apply if Matthew really experienced what you have told me.' Margaret replaced the book on the shelf. 'Matt experienced *something*… something beyond his normal appreciation of events, that's for sure. Whether it was a psychometric moment or not remains to be seen. We can check – if Lyle did what Matthew says he did…' She left the rest in the air.

Adam's fingers played a tattoo on the glass case. 'Frightening…' he said.

'Only one thing frightens me,' said Margaret. 'Suppose it all happened just as Matt described…'

Adam jiggled the tracing paper, trying to improve on Margaret's positioning of it over the fragments of the clay disc.

Margaret murmured, 'The design on a clay amulet belonging to Dai. The children made a tracing of it…' while still thinking of the problems thrown up by Matthew's psychic tricks. 'Remember the poor old barber-surgeon? The one who was crushed to death by the falling sarsen?'

Adam suddenly realised that the pace of events was snowballing fast…

Margaret lifted the glass case and took out the mounted fragments of clay disc. 'These bits were found by his body…'

The blackness was complete. An old velvet obscurity which could be touched. But for Dai, the very smell of the darkness was comfort and the assurance that all was well in his world.

The spark exploded and the match was immediately cupped and coaxed with minor blasphemies, flaring into life, catching the bright gleam of the old hermit's eye. The dried bracken crackled and spat, the twigs twisted and charred, a woodlouse hurried blindly from beneath the bark of a rotten log, and Dai's supper was under way…

The shadow of the pot danced along the walls, the flames colouring the dim niches of stone with green and orange, the only light they had ever seen.

Dai warmed his body at the fire and sniffed appreciatively at the mess within the pot. Something missing, yet. He reached up into the darkness and delicately dragged some wild garlic out of a drying bunch. He crushed the herb between horny fingers and tossed it into the pot, wiped his fingertips on his top lip, breathing in the promise of food, the smells of life.

From another spike the blood dropped from a cock pheasant, too fresh, too newly dead. 'Another day. Another two,' muttered the old reprobate, savouring the gamey thought. He smiled his frayed, brown-toothed smile and his rheumy fox-eyes cracked down to the merest slits as he saw the worn bone toys lying beside his sleeping nest of tattered blankets. The bones of a rabbit, handled and worn smooth with affection, they ruled his actions. Daily, ten times a day, they directed his hunting, told him to rest, reminded him of plans forgotten… the augurers of Rome had forecast joy and disaster with such bones. Dai's existence depended upon what they foretold…

He rattled them in his hands and casually threw them on the rock. They landed in a shape he had not seen before.

'Never the same, never the same.' He squatted over them and the fire flared for him to see their meaning.

The pattern they made was not immediately obvious... but the shock as realization came was all the more for that reason. Dai felt the chill begin at the base of his spine. His legs began to quiver and as he leaned forward to sweep the bones up in one great calloused hand, a bead of ice-cold sweat trickled down the side of his face.

He waited. As the moment came he threw the bones again... the tiny skull rolled and seemed never to want to come to rest... until it struck the last of the bones and lay grinning obscenely up at the frightened old man. 'Never the same, never the same,' protested Dai drily as the fear struck again. But this time, the bones were the same... the very same... zigzagging back from the skull in the shape of the Winged Serpent...

A low growl grew in his throat, involuntarily. His knees gave way beneath the weight of fear, and his hands stretched out to the bones to scrabble them into another shape, any other shape...

The fire leaped and a log cracked and began to roar. The ancient stones of the burial chamber moved in the light. Carved faces laughed at the old frightened man who knew that somewhere in the barrow, beyond the reach of the firelight, the same representation of the Winged Serpent, drawn there in primordial times, was waiting, watching, warning...

Dai sweated in his blankets, not knowing how to still his terror. The amulet gave no ease, for now its power seemed dead... Dai shook with a dread he could not control.

From outside the barrow, a high fluting voice with sunlight in it penetrated the entrance defences, pierced the darkness of the stone passage, and reached for Dai through the flaring firelight and steam from the pot...

'Dai...'

Again, urgently, 'Dai... are you there?'

Dai clamped his hands over his ears and squirmed further beneath his bedding, shutting out the present, keeping out the future. His eyes tried to crack the darkness of the passageway apart, tried to wrench away the timbers and boulders which blocked the entrance to the barrow, tried desperately to let in the promised rescue of that voice but not the fear of its message.

Something fluttered white in the dim recesses of the passage, a piece of paper fell like a dying moth from a crevice in the guarding entrance timbers. Dai found the strength of curiosity in his legs and crawled out of his nest and through the steam to the scrap of paper. The crude drawing of a broken bicycle opened his mind again...

His voice the merest croak, praying that he was right, 'Matthew? Is that Matthew...?'

A bubble of laughter. Again that fluting voice, 'Dai? Yes, Dai... Matthew's here...'

The girl. Sandra. Matthew's friend.

The old man tore away the first of the timbers, enough to let the outside in...

Sandra beamed at him through the gap. 'My mother wants to see that clay thing with the serpent on it.'

She climbed through, followed by Matthew.

Relief did not blind the old man's foxy brain. 'Well, she can't. It's mine.'

Kevin appeared in the entrance to the barrow. Behind him, the dark of the sun outlined his figure, left him faceless...

The fear returned.

'Why did he come? Why did you bring that...?'

Matthew turned to see what it was that scared his old friend. Kevin moved into the passage. 'Don't be silly, Dai. He's one of us...'

Dai almost sniffed at the boy, all his senses alert, knife-edged. 'Are you, boy?' It was an accusation.

'I don't know what you mean.' Kevin smiled, disarmingly.

Dai could not let go. There was a smell of evil here.

The scent of death...

Kevin said, quietly, persuasively, 'Give me the amulet, Dai. Give it to me…'

The poacher drew away from the young into the shadows, pressed himself into the rock of the passage wall, and plunged his hand protectively into the pocket containing the amulet. 'You'd like that, wouldn't you? You'd like me to go unprotected?' He wheezed, short of breath, cold fear gripping again. 'Never… it came to me… it's mine…'

The clay disc leaped in his hand, turned fully over, crumbled into many pieces and its power fled.

Dai drew the pieces disbelievingly from his pocket and stared down at them, lying in his hand. From deep inside himself a feeling arose and uttered itself as a primitive cry of despair. Staggering, stumbling, he moved along the wall, past the ancient carving of the Winged Serpent, out of the barrow, out of the Sanctuary, into the day and oblivion.

Matthew and Sandra broke after him.

Leaving behind Kevin, smiling his happy smile…

CHAPTER NINE

MARGARET POURED THE COFFEE into the earthenware mug that she had begun to think of as 'Adam's' and took it across to where he was leaning over the display containing the model of the modern village.

'Fifty-three stones remaining... fifty-three leylines plotted for the Circle...' He burned his fingers on the hot mug and placed it quickly on the glass of the case. 'Invisible power cables...'

She spooned brown sugar into her own coffee. 'Don't tell me you are coming to believe in it all...? I thought you scientists needed proof?'

Adam made a noncommittal noise. 'There are more things in heaven and earth than are philosophised about in my dreams...'

She looked at the back of his head as he sipped at his drink, the way the black hair curled over his collar. He needed a haircut. She smiled.

'Fifty-three,' he pondered. 'Is it a significant number?'

'Five and three were both supposed to be sacred numbers...' Margaret's voice trailed away. Adam looked up, expectantly.

'Something?'

Margaret shrugged; it was a crazy coincidence. She hesitated but Adam was waiting. 'Before you and Matthew came, the village had fifty-three inhabitants...'

The doorway darkened and Lyle leaned against the wall outside, beaming with pleasure. 'You'll never believe it, my dear,' he said, 'but I finally remembered your Parker's "Milbury." '

Margaret took the slim green volume gratefully. 'We've been talking of you… Adam's been trying to get hold of you.'

The doctor turned the beam on Adam. 'Nothing professional, I hope?'

Margaret moved to the coffee, started to polish a new mug for the doctor.

Adam realised that by questioning Lyle about his whereabouts last night, he would sound like a detective, at best. At worst, foolish. But what was the alternative? To introduce the subject of Matthew's clairvoyant experiences, it would be necessary first to establish Lyle's actual movements.

The moment was embarrassing and one not to be relished. Head first was the only way…

'Doctor… what happened to you last night?'

Lyle's good-natured grin faded for a moment. He seemed genuinely puzzled. 'You know what happened to me…'

Impasse. Adam hung on. 'So you saw your old patient… thirty-odd miles away?'

Lyle frowned. 'Yes.'

'No problems on the way?' This was ridiculous… Adam could feel his colour rising under Lyle's amused regard. 'Your car didn't break down?'

'Any reason why it should?'

Adam hesitated. 'Forgive me, it's just that… Matthew had this absurd idea. He thought he could feel what was happening to you, you see…'

Lyle stopped smiling. This *was* professional, then… 'Feel?'

Adam produced the doctor's gloves. 'Through these. You left them behind.'

Although delighted to see his gloves again, Lyle still seemed nonplussed.

Margaret handed him a mug of coffee. 'Psychometry,' she said.

The doctor was at home immediately; this was something that he could understand. And with interest, too. 'So Matt's a budding psychometrist, is he?'

Adam could finish now. 'He was convinced you were stopped at the edge of the Circle by something barring your way.'

Lyle sipped at the coffee. 'Something in the road, you mean?'

'Yes.' They both said it, Adam and Margaret.

The doctor finished his coffee quickly. 'Well, I'm sorry to disappoint you, but he was wrong.' He smiled.

So did Adam. 'Frankly, I'm relieved. I'm not sure I'd know how to cope with a psychometric son.'

'Bit awkward having him know what you were up to all the time. Well,' Lyle turned in the doorway, 'sorry I couldn't be of help. Happy Day to you.'

Margaret froze as she placed the mug on the desk. Adam felt his blood drain away from his heart. Whitefaced, Margaret whirled on Adam. His head pounded out the dread message…

Happy Day to you… Happy Day to you… Happy Day to you…

Lyle was gone.

The heat shimmer and the springy turf made running a dream process. The harder you tried, the slower you moved. The faster you drove yourself, the less you progressed. Matthew stopped by one of the sarsens in the Avenue and waited for Sandra to catch up. Far behind, Kevin ambled after them, as though there was no hurry. Ahead, Dai ran down the centre of the Avenue like a goat, arms and knees flying, coat flapping, one shoe held in his hand.

Matthew screwed up his eyes against the sun-glare and set off again along the Avenue. The Circle looked far away, as far as when he started from the Sanctuary. Dai stayed ahead, a tiny figure, fleeing into the distance. Behind him, Sandra ran silently, head down, hanging gamely on.

105

Blood pounded in Matthew's head, drowning out his thoughts. His brain raced before him, trying to figure Dai's motives, wondering why his fear carried him so fast. He set himself to catch the old man before he reached the earthwork, but as he looked up again, Matthew saw that it was a hopeless task.

Dai had reached the foot of the high embankment and was climbing fast, hands and knees, scrambling, slipping diagonally toward the top ridge. Matthew stopped. Sandra dropped to a trot, her eyes fixed on the climbing figure.

Dai reached the ridge and turned to look back at Matthew and Sandra. Kevin trotted on, halfway down the Avenue. Dai backed away along the ridge, then turned, stumbled and, in a flurry of arms and legs, fell and disappeared out of sight down the other side of the bank.

Matthew and Sandra ran for the bottom of the earthwork and started climbing toward the point where Dai had fallen. Kevin did not change pace.

Gaining the ridge, Matthew stared down into the ditch on the other side of the earthwork. No sign of Dai. No fallen figure. No one in sight. 'Where's he gone?' gasped Sandra, totally out of breath. Matthew could not answer. Dai had completely disappeared.

'This is where he fell,' said Sandra. 'Exactly here.'

They stared down into the ditch below them. Kevin arrived and joined them. At the point where Dai must have landed at the bottom of the earthwork, within the Circle, lay a fallen sarsen.

On it, weathered by the centuries, but still visible, was a carving of the Solar Serpent.

Matthew burst into the cottage.

Seated at the table, calmly drinking tea, were Mrs Crabtree and Dr Lyle. They looked up, surprised, almost guilty, as though they shared a secret. Mrs Crabtree immediately started clearing the table and bustling the tea things into the kitchen.

Matthew was puzzled by their reactions. Sandra and Kevin arrived in the doorway behind him. 'I'm looking for my father. He's obviously not here?'

The doctor beamed kindly. 'What are you all doing here? Why aren't you at school?'

Matthew ignored him and called into the kitchen, 'Where's my father, Mrs C?'

Lyle said, 'He's at the Museum. I've just come from there.'

Matthew turned to go but suddenly remembered. 'Did he tell you about… ?

'Your experiment in telepathy? He did indeed.'

Matthew was puzzled; the doctor seemed so calm about it all. Surely it was the most exciting and frightening thing that had ever happened… 'What was it that you saw at the edge of the Circle?' asked Matthew.

Lyle hardly hesitated. 'I saw an open road.'

'You didn't stop at all?'

That smile again. 'I'm afraid not.'

Matthew stared at the doctor, trying to get past that smile. 'The picture was so clear.'

Sandra tugged at his shirt. Dai… there were more important things to do than to stand chatting mysteriously with the doctor.

Lyle moved toward Matthew and only half-humorously suggested, 'Perhaps I'd better take another look at that cracked head of yours.'

Matthew and Sandra got to the door as Kevin said, 'Here, wait for me…'

Matthew blocked the doorway and stared at Kevin and Lyle. Both were smiling. Something inside his head stirred and he heard himself saying, 'It's time you got to school.' It was only as he said it that he realised the truth of what he was saying. 'I'm sure Miss Clegg will be happy to see you.'

As Matthew and Sandra went, Lyle smiled at Kevin and said, 'He's quite right, you know. She will be happy…'

Matthew and Sandra flew down the village street.

'Think he's been got at?' called Sandra.

Matthew avoided a parked bike. 'Dai knew it… good enough for me…'

'But how did Dai know?'

'Dunno,' puffed Matthew. He'd never run so far since his last cross-country. 'But why was the doctor at the cottage?'

Sandra took the corner. 'Talking to old Crabface.'

'Right. That's something he wouldn't have done yesterday…'

Sandra forked hard across the road and into the Post Office. Matthew stopped himself by grabbing a passing telegraph pole. Surprised, he followed her.

Mrs Warner peered through her wire grille as Sandra took a postcard out of the rack and handed it to Matthew.

It was a photograph of the font in the church and the carving of the Winged Serpent was plainly visible, as Margaret had said. The design was also identical to the one on Dai's disc, the barber-surgeon's amulet remains, and the carving on the rock at the spot where Dai fell… the Solar Serpent…

'This, I want to see,' said Matthew.

'You can't. The church is locked.'

'But why?'

Sandra shook her hair away from her eyes, 'Because there's no priest, no vicar… there hasn't been for ages.'

Matthew examined the postcard carefully, even read the small print on the back.

'Mum says it's up to Mr Hendrick. It's one of those old churches where the priest is appointed by the Lord of the Manor.' Sandra waited while Matthew pondered his next move.

He went to the counter and showed the card to Mrs Warner. 'Six pence, I think.'

She had been interested ever since Sandra had chosen the postcard, craning her scraggy old neck in an effort to see what it was that the young girl had chosen, unable quite to overhear their muted conversation. She reacted very oddly to the card that Matthew showed her. 'I'm sorry, Matthew. That's not for sale.' And her scarlet fingernails flashed out and snatched the card from his surprised hand.

Sandra protested, 'But it was in the rack, marked 6p.'

A wintry smile. 'My mistake, it's not for sale.'

And she resolved the situation by melting away through the door behind the grille that led to her private apartments. As she went Matthew imagined that he heard her say, quite cheerfully, 'Happy Day, children...'

In the Museum, Margaret studied a chart of the village which showed the present position of every known sarsen. She looked up at Matthew and Sandra with astonishment. 'But there *is* no stone there. If it was a sarsen it would be marked on this chart.'

'But we saw it,' Matthew protested feebly. He was beginning to doubt even the evidence of his senses. 'Could it be marked on some other chart? After all, it's the only stone I've seen that's not been re-erected.'

Margaret stared at Matthew thoughtfully. 'Wait a moment.' She moved across the floor to the barber-surgeon display and pointed to a photomural of the earthwork which backed the glass case. Her finger indicated a general area: 'Would X mark the spot?'

Excitedly, Matthew recognised the layout of the land and the impression of the Avenue stretching away in the background.

'It's impossible.' Margaret shook her head, troubled. 'That's the place where the barber-surgeon was found. Crushed to death by a fallen sarsen.'

There was a real silence in the room now.

Sandra, white, said, 'That must be the one we saw, then.' But she did not sound as though she believed herself.

They all looked at each other. Here, they were leaving the realms of the possible and entering a world that they had not ventured into before.

Margaret did not need to say it but the words tumbled out, despite herself. 'The rock was removed years ago and re-erected in the Circle... there's nothing there now...'

CHAPTER TEN

ADAM LED THE OTHERS through the village. Each of them struggled with the confusion of thoughts thrown up by the sequence of events of the day so far. The sun threw long morning shadows still and yet so much had happened. Most important of all, to Dai. His behaviour when he had broken his talisman, his subconscious realization that Kevin had been 'Happy-Dayed,' his fall and disappearance worried Matthew, who had no wish to lose yet another friend. Lyle's behaviour over that glove business reinforced Adam's belief that, in some way, Matthew had been right in his psychometric experience; but without knowing exactly what had happened to the doctor and his son last evening there was no way of telling for sure how they had been 'got at,' as Sandra put it. He only knew that somewhere, Hendrick had a hand in it, but how and why remained a mystery. Perhaps *the* mystery.

The Circle curved away in the sunlight, old and yet new and surprising each time. There were meanings in the relationship of each stone to the next, Matthew felt sure, but meanings hidden in the mind of the priests who originated the project, centuries ago.

If only in some way he could enter into the mind of such a priest… maybe through his pyschometric trick… a frightening thought.

Matthew aimed slightly right of the line Adam was taking across the centre of the Circle and the others adjusted their steps to follow. Matthew knew that the fallen sarsen was in the ditch exactly in line with the Avenue beyond. Adam joined him at his shoulder and grinned; the excitement was mounting in the little group. Matthew grinned back at his father; it felt almost like a race to find the sarsen first…

They were almost in a line as they came to the edge of the inner ditch and looked down. The great earthwork towered beyond the ditch and the sun, still low, threw a heavy shadow down to where the sarsen should have been…

Margaret gasped, almost as though she knew what she was going to see. She wound her arms protectively about Sandra and tried to turn her daughter's head, so that she would not see the dreadful sight.

Adam watched Matthew carefully out of the corner of his eye. The boy turned pale but there had been a certain inevitability about this discovery, a certain knowledge somewhere inside him that this was what he would find… at the bottom of the ditch, deep in the shadow of death, were the crushed remains of his friend, Dai.

Adam and Matthew slid carefully down into the morning dark. From beside the body, Dai looked like a bundle of old rags. There was nothing that reminded Matthew of his friend. Adam reached forward gingerly and gathered together a few objects. He stared down into his hand at them, turning them over and over. Without a word, he handed them to his son. They were the fragments of Dai's disc… like Dai, there was no life in them. The boy realised suddenly how cold it was out of the sun.

Highfield House had the nearest telephone, Adam decided. Hendrick's house. He cut fast across the Circle. The great stone house came nearer, its twisted chimneys high above the surrounding walls. Adam saw a narrow door set in the wall and tried it. Creaking, it gave a little and he realised he was looking into a beautifully tended kitchen garden. The door would only open a few inches but was being held shut by a pile of seed trays and roof tiles, the sort of day-to-day debris of an old house. He put his back to the door and kept pushing until the old oak opened enough to let him squeeze through.

He hurried along the gravel path to the wrought-iron gate on the far side of the vegetable plots. Suddenly the house was close; he had saved minutes by not going around to the main gates. Adam sprinted across the lawn and stopped under a great cypress which looked as old as the house. The gardens were deserted but a face at the first-floor window was watching him... a gaunt suave face, impassive and disturbing.

He pulled at the bell of the main door and far within the house he heard movement. Footsteps approached without hurry and Adam pounded his fist against the iron-studded oak. The great door slowly swung back and the tall figure of Link, Hendrick's manservant, stood aside to let him in.

'Hendrick? Is he here?'

'I will see, sir.' The door closed on well-oiled hinges.

'Come on, man. It's urgent.' Adam was conscious of looking fraught and dishevelled. 'Where's your phone?' He cast his eye around the panelled hall.

'If you'll just wait here, sir...' The manservant shimmered away into the recess of the house.

Adam, totally alone, felt some of the urgency drain away. It required an effort of will on his part to ignore the polished luxury of the fine house and the aura of calm and content that it displayed. The fine old Tompion longcase startled him out of his reverie as it started the whirring that led to its chiming the quarter hour. Adam checked it against his watch and caught sight of its counterpart on the high mantel. A digital electronic timekeeper flickered eight-figure information while looking utterly out of place.

The telephone stood on the bureau and Adam grabbed the receiver and dialled 999.

Hendrick appeared, pleasantly expansive. 'Adam... what a pleasant surprise.'

Nothing much was happening on the telephone. Unsure what ringing tone, if any, a countryside village could supply for its emergency services, Adam hung on for a moment. The phone did not feel 'dead'... it was simply that nothing was happening. Adam was beginning to feel slightly foolish in his man-of-action guise. He had better explain himself. 'There's a man – that Welsh poacher – he's dead.'

Hendrick's smile slipped for a second. 'Dead? Are you sure?'

'Of course I'm sure. I've just seen his body... by the earthwork... it appears to have been crushed... by some enormous force...'

Hendrick frowned. 'An accident?'

Adam beat at the receiver rest and muttered into the unresponding telephone. He waved it at Hendrick questioningly.

Ignoring Adam, Hendrick collapsed into a comfortable armchair and shook his head wonderingly. 'Poor old Dai... still there's no escaping one's destiny, is there?' He smiled up at Adam's puzzlement. 'Remember that poem of Francis Thompson's?

"I fled Him down the nights and down the days;

I fled Him down the arches of the years;

I fled Him down the labyrinthine ways

Of my own mind: and in the midst of tears

I hid from Him, and under running laughter..." '

Still smiling, he said, 'There's no escape, is there?'

Adam replaced the receiver. 'We ought to inform the police. Where's the nearest station?'

For a long moment Hendrick stared into the empty fireplace, as though wondering what to do; then lightly and quickly he moved across the room and picked up the telephone receiver. He jiggled the rest. 'Police? My dear fellow...' With his smile, he should have been in politics. 'I don't think we need involve them, do you? What if he died of natural causes? We'll get hold of Dr Lyle.' He replaced the receiver with finality and turning, said kindly, 'I'm afraid you didn't have an outside line...'

114

Adam stood his ground. There was something amiss here. 'The police will have to be told.'

Hendrick took his arm comfortably and familiarly, easing him gently toward the door. 'I'll tell you what… let's go and take a look, make sure we're not making any mistake…'

There could be no mistake, Adam was certain of that. Dai was dead.

At the door Hendrick let Adam lead the way into the brightness of the sunlit morning, saying, 'As the local JP, I suppose I represent the majesty of the law in Milbury…'

Margaret and Sandra walked slowly ahead of Matthew between the stones. It was difficult to comprehend the meaning that lay behind the series of events that was driving them all toward an unknown area. Matthew was aware in his own mind that the circle of life around himself and his father was narrowing quickly, too quickly to understand, far too quickly for comfort.

Matthew glanced again at the fragments of Dai's talisman, which he felt held the answer…

He heard Margaret say, 'Let me get this straight. You saw Dai fall from the earthwork? And when you got there, he'd disappeared?'

'There was just a fallen stone. With a serpent carved on it…'

They were nearing the village now, passing the last great sarsen. 'A serpent like the one on the amulet?' asked Margaret.

Sandra tossed her hair back nervously. 'Exactly the same. The same as on the barber-surgeon's clay disc, the same as on the font in the church…'

Matthew stopped as though he had been struck. Staring at the towering stone, he pointed to the unmistakable mark upon it… 'And exactly the same as that…'

Sandra and Margaret followed his pointing finger. Carved deeply into the rock was the symbol of the Winged Serpent…

The sun died behind a cloud.

As the manservant descended the great staircase, the silence of the house was broken only by the ticking of the longcase clock. He stopped and opened the brass bevel, ignoring the whirring sound that indicated an impending chime and keeping his eyes on the digital clock over the mantel. The figures flickered to the hour, and he moved the great minute hand back a fraction to agree exactly with its modern counterpart.

Closing the glass face again, the tall figure moved off into the servants' quarters with the satisfied smile of a job well done.

Adam shivered in the sudden gloom. The day had darkened perceptibly, and the breeze that had carried the sweet morning sharpness was now chilling.

Hendrick, moving gracefully for a man of his size, led the way up the slight rise to the lip of the inner ditch.

The empty inner ditch.

Adam took a beat before the realization struck home. The ditch was empty. No crushed body. No great stone. Just thickish grass still wet with dew.

'Perhaps this isn't the place?' Hendrick did not sound as though he believed himself.

Grimly, Adam checked his line. 'This is the place, all right…'

Hendrick smiled. 'Come now, this is a civilised community. We're not bodysnatchers.'

Adam slid down the face of the ditch, down where the sparkle of the morning had turned damp and rank. Carefully he parted the grass at the place where he had found Dai… Exactly at the spot, hardly visible, covered with moss and lichens, was a low rock outcrop with roughly the same contours as a small, scraggy, spread-eagled body…

Trying hard to keep his justification out of his voice, Adam shouted up to Hendrick, 'He was here. And this rock wasn't…'

'So what are you suggesting?' asked the astronomer. 'Someone removed him and put the rock in his place?' He laughed gently at the absurdity.

Adam stared down at the buried boulder. 'I'm not suggesting anything,' he said, more or less to himself. 'I just don't understand it…'

Hendrick turned away, high above him, a big figure dark against the sky. 'Well, anyway, old man… he obviously wasn't dead…'

The boulder appeared on Matthew's painting. It took him some time to realise that the rock depicted was at the very spot where Dai had tumbled from the earthwork but allowed for small differences in perspective… His heart leaped with excitement. 'Here it is… that rock we saw. Where we found Dai. There's something in the picture.'

Margaret and Sandra crowded over his shoulder and searched the painting. Matthew pointed to the spot. Margaret checked quickly with a chart showing the present position of the stones.

There was no stone marked for that position, nothing at all in the ditch area.

'But look,' Matthew compared the painting with the chart. 'The one we saw on the way back… the sarsen with the serpent carved on it… it isn't painted into the picture.'

Sandra puzzled, 'But it *is* marked on the chart…'

They stared at each other, minds whirling.

Margaret was the first to give up the struggle to comprehend the wheeling possibilities that the Circle seemed to be presenting in confusion. 'Matt, how many figures are there in the painting?'

This was a new track, the aim of which was not at all apparent to Matthew. He shook his head. 'No idea…'

Margaret's voice was urgent. 'Count them…'

The manservant opened the great oak door, and Hendrick entered. 'Nothing untoward, I trust, sir? The gentleman seemed quite agitated.'

Hendrick grunted with amusement. 'You know what these scientists are, Link. Always looking for rational explanations.'

Link's face cleared. 'So things are as they should be?'

Deep in the armchair, Hendrick made a decision. 'I shall be having another dinner party tonight.'

The manservant raised his eyebrows but did not speak.

'The sooner we are all one big happy family, the better,' smiled his master.

'There are four to choose from, sir. Four who haven't yet enjoyed your hospitality. You'll invite them all together?'

'No, no.' Hendrick considered. 'They must come in order of precedence.'

Link smiled down at his master. 'So it's the ladies first?'

Hendrick smiled back. 'Precisely.'

'Fifty-five.' The words tumbled out of Matthew. 'There are fifty-five people in the picture.'

Margaret said softly, 'I thought there might be.' Seeing Matthew's slight surprise, she explained, 'Now that you and your father have arrived, there are fifty-five people in the village.'

Sandra broke in, 'But the artist can't have known that.'

'No…' Margaret tried to word her next phrase carefully, 'But it's almost as if…'

The door opened and Adam came into the Museum. They all turned to him but the thought continued, despite Adam's obviously troubled manner.

'As if what, Mum?'

'As if that painting was some sort of… prophecy.'

The moment hung in the air. Adam smashed it to the ground with his next words. 'It's gone. Dai's body. It's gone. Disappeared.'

Matthew's brain danced. 'So he wasn't dead.' Denying the evidence of his eyes, Matthew's hope leaned toward the impossible.

'He was dead,' said his father, grimly. 'I'm no doctor but he was dead.' He watched his son admit the truth of his words but the hope lingered in the boy's eyes.

Matthew took the broken pieces of the clay disc out of his pocket and put them on the table before him during the silence. He moved them about, trying to repair the pattern. Suddenly he tightened. 'Dad... look...'

The boy moved over to the barber-surgeon display case and slid back the protective glass screen. Margaret hurried across to him. 'What do you need, Matt?'

'The fragments... the amulet.'

She took out the circular mounting which contained the remains of the clay disc and gave it carefully into the boy's hands. Matthew placed it on the table, and taking a piece of Dai's disc tried to match it in a gap in the mounted fragments... It fitted perfectly.

Sandra whistled through her teeth.

'Go on, Matt,' Adam urged. 'Try the others.'

Matthew chose a smaller piece and slipped it into the ancient jigsaw... and another, and another. Excitedly he tried to complete the disc. The clay pieces did not even vary in colour, and the breaks between the segments hardly showed.

The final piece slotted into place and Matthew snatched his hands away in pain and surprise.

He stared miserably at his father.

Adam felt his dismay. 'This too?'

Matthew nodded dumbly. He was afraid. Afraid of the responsibility. Afraid of what he had re-created. Afraid of the confirmation that this might give of Dai's death. But he knew too that there was no way in which he could avoid the investigation of the amulet, no way in which he could deny the amulet the opportunity of communicating through him...

He took the disc and mounting into his hands.

Adam, worried, said, 'Take care, Matt,' without knowing how that could be done.

Matthew tightened his fingers into the surface of the completed disc, into the body and heart of the Solar Serpent... the pain immediately sweetened into sound and the light came...

'Yes... the static... the energy... it's there...'

Sandra was frightened by the ghastly change in Matthew. She half-screamed as his staring eyes rolled up unseeing into their sockets.

Margaret held her daughter tightly.

'Visitor...'

He hardly made himself heard, his voice was secondary to the sense. Perhaps it was not his voice... later, no one could be sure what it was they heard.

Adam had some such thought beating in his head. He took a pencil and scribbled... Visitor.

'Visitor...' again.

Matthew understood. Everything. The meaning and life of the Circle. Reason and sense manifest. The stars coursed through his existence with the aching power of knowledge. No darkness entered the light of his mind. No death waited for the end of things. Only peace and... and... and... sound... That fine purity of matter resolved into silver sound... turning to pain, slipping upwards into agony... the twisting shock of nerves drawn through steel into blackness... and the loss... the loss... He stared around him.

Margaret took the disc mounting from his trembling hand. Suddenly, his legs went and Adam lifted him to a chair.

'Dad... what happened... what did I see?'

Adam held him close. He wiped away the sweat from his face with his hand. 'Do you remember, Matt? What you saw?'

Matthew searched among the loss but all was dark. 'Nothing... I remember nothing.'

'You spoke. You said words.' Adam handed Matthew the notebook and the words floated before him. He waited for them to trigger his mind back to that wonderful and terrifying place, but they were powerless pencillings on paper.

Beginning… he read. End… Visitor… Bright… Shining… Circle… People… Village… Priest… Stones… Power… Always… Always…

Meaningless words.

He looked at his father and tried a grin. 'Pick the bones out of that, then.'

Adam grinned back. 'We *must* pick the bones out of that… that's all we've got.' He re-read the jottings.

'Visitor… Someone visiting the village?'

'The priest, perhaps,' suggested Margaret. 'A visiting priest?'

'Stones… Power… Always…' Adam shrugged. 'Always power in the stones… that makes sense. But "bright shining circle"?…'

Matthew was glancing at the painting. 'It's not the circle that's bright and shining,' he said slowly. 'It's something else.'

'The priest?' prompted Margaret.

'Or the visitor.' Adam frowned.

Sandra felt she had to say something. 'A visitor, bright and shining?' It sounded like something from a fairytale.

Adam leaped on the thought. 'Wait a minute. Visitor… guest.'

They waited. His excitement bubbled and he fought hard to control it, to keep cool the workings of his intellect. 'A guest star. That's what it used to be called in the old days…'

His excitement was infectious. 'Explain,' said Margaret. 'What was called a guest star?'

As he answered, Adam wished that the thought had never come to him… 'A supernova.' The words died in his mouth.

They stared at each other with a fear which was only now being born within them but which they knew would grow into the beast that would devour them if they found no avenue of escape…

Hendrick's Supernova… the black hole.

CHAPTER ELEVEN

HENDRICK PORED OVER HIS astrochart, making calculations on the edge of the paper and transferring the results to his notepad. He ripped out the page as Link entered.

'Whisky and water, sir?'

'No, I'll have one at the pub.' Hendrick handed over the page of jottings. 'Run these through the computer, will you? Usual program.' He hesitated and frowned. 'I hope I've got those correlations right.'

'You've never been wrong yet, sir.'

Hendrick looked at Link with distaste. 'I can't afford to be wrong.' He thought further and made some more calculations on his pad. 'When did we transmit last night?'

'Conjunction was at 2033 hours 42.75 seconds, sir.'

The astronomer compared his latest figures with this information and said, 'Then if those figures make sense, tonight we'll start at…?'

Link smiled reassuringly at his master and flourished the page of figures that he had been given. 'I'll call you to dinner in good time, sir.'

Hendrick felt that in some way, he was being patronised by his manservant. Link noticed his edginess and hurriedly said, 'I'll run these right away, sir.' They both left the room, taking their tensions with them.

At the pub, Adam and Margaret stared gloomily into their drinks. The babble of inane twitter that passes for conversation at such a time was heavy enough to isolate them in their corner. Adam scowled even harder. 'Beginning. End. Circle. Always. A never-ending Circle…?'

Margaret waited. The lines around his eyes were from laughter years, those around his mouth from the time of recent pain. It was those silly frown lines at the bridge of his nose she loved so much. Such concentration…

'As far as I can make out,' he said, 'that's the beginning and the end.' He smiled at his pathetic joke.

'Well, it sounded genuine enough, Matthew's utterance. He certainly seems to have the gift.'

'That's what worries me.' The frown returned. 'I think he really did see Lyle through those gloves. I think he saw him drive away and stop at the edge of the Circle. Next day, Lyle starts "Happy Daying" us all. The question is…' He sank his Scotch. 'What happened to him in between?'

Margaret wanted so much to believe the doctor's story but… 'He says he went to visit his patient, thirty miles away. He says.'

'And came back a different man?' Adam shook his head. 'Don't forget Kevin's changed too.'

They were silent, surrounded by noise.

'So whatever it was, happened here…?' Margaret mused. 'Inside the Circle.' There was little doubt that he was right but the thought did nothing to lift their pocket of gloom.

Across the bar, Adam caught sight of Hendrick paying for his drink. Seeing that Margaret was almost finished, Adam muttered, 'Here's Hendrick… drink up, I don't want to corner him until I've thought this through.'

They got almost to the door before the well-known voice greeted them. 'Too late to buy you a drink?' The astronomer beamed at them both, charming and affable.

Not wishing to seem churlish, Adam went through the good-neighbour rigmarole of nodding and smiling and 'Thanks but no thanks, we're just going.' But then his curiosity overcame his good sense and he decided that there was a question that Hendrick could be tackled about. 'That clay disc in the Museum... the barber-surgeon's amulet... what connection could that have with your supernova?'

Hendrick stared. The question had obviously come right out of the blue, and it seemed to confuse him.

Adam gave him time, then said, 'Matthew thinks they are connected, but he can't figure how...'

'Does he now? Perceptive boy, that son of yours. Perceptive and formidable...'

A parry, Adam decided. It was certainly no answer of any sort. Hendrick's undoubted charm was a good deal more than skin deep, and Adam, despite himself, could not help liking the man. But the smile gave nothing away. Always supposing, he grudgingly conceded, that there was anything to give away. He found himself making goodbye noises and ushering Margaret out into the relative certainty of the gathering afternoon.

The barrow was deserted, the entrance just as they had left it. Almost two hours they waited there, hoping against hope that Dai would in some miraculous way appear. Matthew knew that he was fooling himself with a dreamer's need but it was difficult to accept the loss of Dai.

Sandra waited because Matthew waited and because she could not understand the sequence of events that had led to Dai's disappearance. Maybe the barrow, the ancient burial place, would provide an answer.

The larks sang but that was the only song they learned.

On the way back along the Avenue they retraced their steps as nearly as possible. At the top of the earthwork, peering down into the ditch but not daring to approach the low, half-buried boulder that they could just make out, Matthew said, 'He's never going back there. I know it now. He's never going back to the Sanctuary.'

Sandra shivered. Was it only this morning that she had last stood here? 'Then where is he?'

'Gone.' Matthew sounded savage. 'Not dead. Just not here any more… I felt that from the disc…' He turned away. 'It's no good, I can't explain.'

At the cottage, Matthew cheered up considerably at the thought of food. He was in the midst of building a couple of his sandwich specials (mint jelly, apple crumble, mayonnaise and ham) when Mrs Crabtree appeared and tried to persuade him to eat 'properly,' as she put it.

She watched as Matthew constructed his desecration. It was her horror as he added the onion and potato crisps to the mess that prompted her to leave the kitchen saying, 'You're not to spoil Miss Sandra's appetite now, Master Matthew. She's going out to dinner tonight.'

The remark half-registered with Matthew, although Sandra had no idea what the silly old hag was referring to… The real problem was, a fried egg to top off with? Or just plain strawberries?

It was only later that evening, when Adam and Matthew were giving Margaret and Sandra a pre-supper drink, that the remark echoed somewhere at the back of Matthew's consciousness. He repeated what Mrs Crabtree had said.

Margaret immediately started worrying about this new development. 'But how did she know? Hendrick hadn't even invited us then.'

Adam saw her concern and quickly grabbed the opportunity. 'Don't go. Tell him you've changed your mind.'

Woman to the last, Margaret smiled and said, 'But I'm longing to see the house…'

They all laughed, needing to loosen the tensions but aware of the realities. Adam kept on, 'Lyle said Hendrick invited him to dinner but he had to refuse because of an appointment with a patient thirty miles away. I don't believe he kept the appointment. So where did he go?'

Sandra stopped admiring her full-length dress for a moment. 'He can't have gone to Mr Hendrick's, not if he wasn't expected…'

'Wasn't he?' Adam was labouring the point. 'If whatever happened to him happened in the village, it could have been at Hendrick's place.'

Margaret tried to laugh away his fears. 'It could have happened anywhere.'

'Hendrick seems to be in charge,' Adam insisted. 'People look up to him. I'm sure he knows what's going on.'

Margaret stood and prepared to leave. She looked beautiful in her long black dress, young and exquisite. 'Then I'll be able to ask him, won't I?' She pretended a confidence she was not too sure she had.

Adam made her promise to come back to the cottage after she had finished dining with Hendrick. A nightcap to reassure him that all was well…

As Sandra rose from the chesterfield, Matthew casually sneaked away a scarf that she had worn over her head when she arrived. Adam noticed his son tucking the small square of silk away under a cushion but could not imagine what it was that Matthew was trying to achieve.

When the girls were gone Adam demanded an explanation. Why on earth should Matthew want to steal Sandra's scarf?

Matthew protested, 'I only borrowed it.'

'But it doesn't suit you.'

They both laughed, then Matthew, rather self-consciously, for it was a far-out idea that he had, told his father, '… to use as a camera.'

Adam's face went through several changes of expression almost simultaneously: admiration at his son's ingenuity, delight at the thought that they would have some knowledge of what was happening at Highfield House, and worry at the thought of what Matthew was going to have to go through to achieve his object.

Grudgingly, he said, 'Clever old you.'

Matthew grinned back, reassuringly. 'Clever *young* me.'

The scarf was wound around Matthew's left fist rather tentatively. Adam said worriedly, 'Perhaps it should be held in your right hand. The left hand has always been associated with evil…'

Matthew shook his head. 'This is the hand I had Dr Lyle's glove on…'

They looked at each other, both realizing that it was the evil they needed to know about, but neither liking to say so. The whole involvement was too frightening…

'Be careful, Matt…'

Hendrick watched Link fixing him a drink. He glanced at the digital clock on the mantel and his mouth set. 'They're late. That's the one thing I didn't allow for…'

'Plenty of time in hand, sir.'

Hendrick snorted. 'Women. Delightful creatures but punctuality is not among their virtues.'

Link realised that his master was unduly nervous tonight. He hurried over with the glass set on a small silver salver. 'There is much, sir, to be said for a celibate life.'

The astronomer took the whisky and stared at Link with a certain distaste. There was a sudden edge to the formality of their relationship. Hendrick tossed back the drink and replaced the glass on the salver. Tired, he looked older and perhaps wiser than before, very much the father figure… 'Yet I have my children…'

And the doorbell rang. Smoothly, Link said, 'The best of both worlds, sir.'

Hendrick immediately relaxed, unwound. 'Here are the new arrivals… I'll receive them. You make sure everything's on schedule…'

Link hurried away as Hendrick opened the great oak door. Framed in the doorway, looking small and delicate against the iron and timber and stone, were Margaret and Sandra.

The astronomer greeted them warmly and apologised for not having invited them to his house before. 'You know what a small village is… one has to observe the protocol.' He was obviously trying his best to make them feel welcome and relaxed.

Margaret and Sandra gazed about them appreciatively and Hendrick smiled when Sandra glanced a second time at the timepiece on the mantel. 'It's a digital clock,' he said. 'Electronic.'

'But what do you need it for? You've got dear old grandfather there…'

'He's handsome, isn't he? Unfortunately he doesn't keep such good time.'

'Much more attractive though,' said Margaret. 'Forgive me but the other looks so…' She shrugged, thinking she had gone too far, questioning the host's taste in clocks.

Hendrick's smile broadened. 'Out of place?' he suggested. 'It's just that I need absolute accuracy for my work. I still dabble… I need to be sure that everything is still where it should be at any given time.'

Margaret suddenly saw something beyond the smile. She tried to see into his eyes but the lids were hooding the truth of his expression. A small shiver of apprehension moved up her spine.

Hendrick's voice grew softer, more caressing. 'The stars and the planets… the other places,' he murmured.

'And your supernova…?' Sandra prompted, brightly.

The astronomer beamed his brilliant smile at her. 'Especially my supernova,' he crooned.

The whole house was suddenly silent.

Matthew bent over his swathed hand but felt nothing.

The scarf had grown warm, almost moist. He began to lose concentration. Adam saw the slight change in attitude and anxiously demanded, 'Well . . ?'

The boy raised his head and smiled. 'Nothing yet. Nothing at all.'

Partly relieved and yet still fearful, Adam considered, 'Perhaps she's not a suitable subject…'

'I don't think it's that,' said Matthew. 'I think anyone's a suitable subject as long as something's happening to them. Something important enough to make them very happy or…'

'Or very otherwise…'

'Yes.' Matthew felt his mouth go acid.

Adam stared at his son, still not sure that he should allow him to live through these experiences but at the same time anxious to know just what was happening at the big house at the centre of the Circle. 'Then let's hope you don't start getting a signal…'

'One thing puzzles me,' said Margaret. She tried to make her voice sound more off-hand, more casual. 'Everyone around here seems to have caught the "Happy Day" bug except you and Dai. How do you explain that?'

Hendrick was imperturbable; he took his time. 'I suppose he and I don't mix as much as others. Haven't picked up the habit.'

Habit? It's true that Dai had never been part of the community in a proper sense, merely a peripheral figure, a raiding pirate on other people's property. The astronomer too could be classed in his role as squire as only a fairly gregarious hermit. But that was not the whole truth…

'People seem to use it as a code. A sign that they share some sort of secret,' said Sandra.

'Aren't you being a little fanciful, my dear?' asked Hendrick. 'It's a local custom, that's all.'

Link arrived silently and announced dinner.

Hendrick glanced at the clocks and rose from his armchair. 'Ready to go up, ladies?'

The girls glanced at each other in surprise. Margaret, rather taken aback, said, 'Up?'

The astronomer offered each of them an arm at the foot of the great staircase and said delightedly, 'Up.'

Matthew glanced up at Adam. 'Felt something then... a sort of tremor...' A pain, dull but aching, remained.

'What was it? Fear?'

'Dunno. It's gone now.' It had nearly gone; just the memory of the agony lingered.

'False alarm?' Adam felt drawn. The waiting had been nerve-wracking for him as much as for Matthew.

'Could be. It was like I felt when Bob wasn't run over by that disappearing lorry.'

They grinned but the worry hung on.

'What an extraordinary room...' Margaret and Sandra stared about them in wonder.

Hendrick had ushered them into a huge circular area at the top of the house. Unplastered stone walls and a great decorated dome above them, the room looked like an uncompleted observatory or camera obscura. In the centre of the space was a round stone table that appeared to be gently dished toward the centre, surrounded by immovable stone seats. In a principal place there was an imposing high-backed seat, ornately carved from a single block of stone. A splendid folly of a room...

Behind them, above the door, another digital clock... Link, bringing up the rear, noted the figures as they flicked to 20:40:00. Exactly on time...

'Not so extraordinary when you consider where we are.' Hendrick waved them to their places. 'Not many have the fortune to live within a stone circle. I wanted the room to reflect this unique environment of ours.'

Link opened a door in the wall but there was no room beyond. The shallow space revealed a kitchen lift and up from below came a heated trolley containing plates and dishes of the food. The manservant wheeled the trolley to a side table, aware of the effect that his conjuring trick was having on the guests. Margaret smiled at him. This was a fascinating house...

As Hendrick took his place at the table, Sandra said, 'Is that a throne?'

The astronomer dipped an exploratory spoon into his soup. 'Found it in a mason's yard,' he said. 'Magnificent, isn't it?'

'And these other pieces – the table and the chairs – you had them made?'

'The mason carved them in the same style from the same stone.'

Margaret's curiosity was racing ahead of her meal. 'Does he do restoration work?' she asked, 'I'm always getting enquiries at the Museum...'

Hendrick shook his head, laughing as though at some private joke. 'Afraid not. He went out of business, ages ago.' He raised his glass to them both in turn and said gently, 'Bon appetit, my children...'

As they responded, Margaret smiled at Hendrick's avuncular mode... 'My children,' indeed. So patronizing.

Adam came from the kitchen with a laden tray. 'Egg and chips do you, Mr Psychometrist?'

'Fantastic.' Matthew had been sitting concentrating on Sandra's scarf which was still wrapped tightly around his left fist. He started to eat one-handed.

'Still quiet out there?' Adam sat at the table.

'No tomato ketchup?'

'Sorry, sir. Coming right up, sir.' Adam sprang to his feet and headed back into the kitchen.

Matthew glanced sharply at the scarf. 'Dad... something's beginning to happen. I can feel it.' The stab of pain from the knife of sound slid sweetly into Matthew's mind... the sound shrilled into light...

Adam hit the RECORD button on the tape-machine which he had standing by on the table and hurriedly pushed the microphone on its stand closer to his son, moving the plate of food to one side.

'Can you see where they are?'

'High... high... at the top of the house...'

Adam puzzled, 'A dining room at the top of the house? Are you sure?'

Matthew's eyes were open but his eyeballs were rolling upwards, only the whites showing. Sweat beaded his brow and the words forced themselves out through the clenched teeth of apparent pain. 'There's a digital clock... it's important... it means something.'

Adam waited. Then, 'Who's there?'

'The girls. Hendrick. And another... a butler...'

'What are they doing?'

Matthew fought away the swirls of darkness that threatened his vision. 'Eating. Just eating. But Sandra's getting nervous...'

The sound of the ancient chant penetrated the stone walls and wormed its way into the room at the top of the house. The rhythms were soft and low but insistent...

Sandra listened hard, trying to catch at the meaning. 'What's that...?'

Hendrick stopped eating and listened. He half-shrugged and went back to his food. 'Villagers. Rather unusual, don't you think? A hymn of celebration...'

Interested by this curious use of the word, under the circumstances, Margaret asked, 'Celebration? What are they celebrating?'

Hendrick's face was shut. He expressed no feeling, no emotion at all as he said, quite seriously, 'Deliverance from the past. Their entry into the future. Now.' The effect of his words was terrifying. The blandness of the astronomer's delivery, together with the import of his simple statement and the growing menace of the chant, somehow conveyed a horror that could not exist. Sandra felt cold creep over her; suddenly it was difficult to breathe.

Link removed the dish from in front of her, and the spell was broken as he knocked over an empty wine glass. Sandra grabbed at it but it was faster than her reflex and rolled down the dished stone into the very centre of the table, out of reach.

The host smiled from his 'throne.' 'Clumsy shape for a table, isn't it?' he said evenly.

Still troubled by the astronomer's explanation of the chant, Margaret muttered in agreement.

'And so it would be if that were its only function…' Hendrick paused for effect. 'Did you know that there was another great dish of stone beneath the ground here?'

Margaret nodded. 'Adam Brake told me that.'

Hendrick's surprise showed momentarily. 'Did he…? Did he also tell you that my house is at the centre of the Circle?'

Sandra chipped in, almost proudly, 'Matthew worked that out. He's very clever at working things out.'

Hendrick smiled at her slowly and very softly said, 'So I've noticed…'

'I still don't see the connection…' Margaret cut across the threat. 'The table and the Circle…'

He half-rose and reached into the centre of the table to retrieve the wine glass. 'Perhaps it is not necessary for you to understand… it is only necessary that you should believe me when I tell you that it all works toward good.' He paused and smiled fondly at Margaret. 'Happiness and peace are the rewards of the believer…'

Margaret shrank back into her seat, fear welling up in her. She reached out and took Sandra's hand. 'You make it sound as if the Circle was a temple and the table an altar.' Sandra hung on tight. '*Your* temple… *your* altar…'

Link coughed discreetly and left the room, closing the door behind him. Hendrick glanced at the digital clock above the closing door and smiled happily at the guests…

Bowing his head, he chanted in time with the sound from outside the house...

'Anger of Fire, Fire of Speech, Breath of Knowledge. Render us free from harm. Return to us the innocence that once we knew. Complete the Circle. Make us at one with nature and the elements.'

He looked up, up into the dome of the room. A section of the ceiling rolled silently back to reveal the night sky.

Hendrick raised his hands and covered his face as he declaimed, 'It is time!'

His throne revolved so that he was left facing the wall, the high back of the seat forming a shield between him and the table...

As Margaret and Sandra stared at each other in frozen terror, unable to move, a shaft of brilliant light rose from the centre of the table and shot through the hole in the dome, into the night. The last thing that the girls knew was the shrilling of the stars and the wind of space as they were irradiated in the glow of the power conjured by their host...

CHAPTER TWELVE

MATTHEW SLUMPED ACROSS THE table, barely conscious. His father grabbed for him, vowing that this was positively the last time that he would allow the boy to endure the agony of his new-found gift, however urgent the reason.

Matthew was pale and trembling in his arms. Adam wiped away the chill of sweat from around his son's eyes. Matthew's brain fought to surface... 'It's gone... there's a blank... a dark... I can't get through any more...'

Adam, despite himself, needed to know more. Needed his fears confirmed. His dread forced him to say, 'Try. You've got to keep trying.' He loathed himself for the pressures he was putting on his son.

The boy shook his head from side to side, his eyes rolling. 'It's no good... she seems to have stopped... feeling...'

'Stopped feeling?' Panic hit Adam hard. 'What's happened to her?'

Matthew was slipping away toward sleep, he struggled against the tide of weariness but he could fight no longer. The room began to turn, slowly at first but accelerating into blackness. His voice whispered in his head, he did not know if his father could hear him... 'No idea... All I know is... she's gone away. We've lost them...'

The sound of space madness died away into the night and the section of the ceiling rolled back into place as Hendrick's throne revolved to face the table again. Sandra was the first to stir but as she pushed herself up from the table, her mother opened her eyes and smiled at her.

Hendrick, more affable than ever, smiled upon them with delight. 'Welcome to you both... how do you feel?' He waited.

Margaret took a moment to reply. There was something... she felt splendid... complete... but something, some sense of loss tugged at her memory. Nothing important, however. She felt no curiosity about what had happened, about this great and generous man who was her host. 'Feel? I feel light... powerful... whole...'

'And happy?' Hendrick's voice caressed.

'Happy? Oh, yes... so happy...'

'So happy...' echoed Sandra.

'Of course.' Hendrick rose. 'Now that you have given... now that you are only good... now you can be happy. Now you are Happy Ones.' He held his hands out over their heads as though in blessing. As they gazed up at him rapturously, he declaimed, 'Go now and take your place... go now and give your thanks... go now and be happy...'

Margaret moved in a dream, floated rather than walked. Her whole being echoed the astronomer's voice as she and Sandra followed Link through the house and into the gardens at the centre of the Circle... Happy... happy... happy...

Surrounding the ancient house was a ring of villagers. Their circle broke as welcoming hands reached out offering them a place in the line of smiling people. Margaret and Sandra moved through the night to their appointed places and the circle reformed and continued to rotate to the rhythm of the chant...

Adam stared into his coffee. Matthew's recovery had been instantaneous and remarkable. The moment sleep had closed his eyes, he had woken. The merest moment of rest had somehow been sufficient to wipe away the effects of his vision. He had recovered his habitual good form and was leaning out of the window listening to the primordial chant coming from the direction of Hendrick's house. Adam's relief at his son's quick recovery blinded him to the turmoil that still had hold of the boy's mind.

Matthew stared into the singing darkness and he was afraid. This was what his friend the poacher had meant. This was the true time of trouble come upon him. An ache was in his heart for the loss of Dai. Very quietly, very much to himself, he called into the night, softly... even he could not hear... 'Dai... where are you, Dai?'

Adam crashed his cup into its saucer and headed for the door. Something must be done about the girls. He could not just sit and wait until things started to happen again. Matthew turned from the window and headed his father off at the door.

'Dad, you can't... don't go out there...'

'Out of the way, I can't just sit here. I must know what's going on.'

Matthew did not move from the doorway. He stared up at his father, puzzled but firm. 'We know what's going on.'

'Then we must try to help.' Adam was close to the tears of frustration. Matthew had never seen his father like this before. Adam saw the worry in the boy's eyes and tried to pull himself together. 'We must try to do something,' he said desperately.

'There's nothing we can do. Nothing we could ever have done. It would have happened anyway... Dai told me. Dai knew. Dai tried to save me, to keep me out of it...'

Adam saw the pain of loss in Matthew's eyes. 'Out of what?' he demanded.

'Whatever it is that we're caught in.' The boy looked as desperate as his father.

Adam moved Matthew physically to one side and wrenched open the door. Driven by his hurt, he risked being callous, anxious to rid his son of what could only be a morbid interest in the dead. 'Dai's gone, Matt. Gone. Forever. Now it's up to us.'

He turned to go into the night but Matthew said quickly, 'It's too late, Dad. It's happened. We're the only ones left.'

Suddenly his son was making sense. The steam went out of his resolve and he hesitated. It was the silence that relit the fire of his determination. The chanting had stopped. The quiet was more frightening than what had gone before.

Adam and Matthew ran through the village night toward the sound of silence...

Highfield House loomed massively at the centre of the Circle. The roofs and twisted brick chimneys were silvered by the moon; the rest of the pile was dark except for the glow of candlelight high in a window at the top of the house.

Crouched beneath the cypress, Matthew whispered, 'That was the room... the one with the flickering light.' As they looked up at the window, the light went out. The house looked dead. Adam touched his son on the shoulder and they turned and left the grounds of the beautiful but frightening place. As they went, they were watched from a darkened window by the pale, staring face of Link.

'Dad? Black holes...'

'What about them?' Adam's voice cut through the clatter of washing up in the kitchen.

'Well, Hendrick's Supernova... it isn't a supernova any more.' Doing two things at once, as usual, Matthew was reading from an astrophysics journal while trying to stack the dishes on the living-room table with the other hand. The article was all about Hendrick's Supernova and the magazine was an old one that Matthew had dug out of his father's jumble of a filing system.

Adam appeared in the kitchen doorway and eyed the supper plates. 'Here, give me those...'

Matthew handed him the stack of dishes, never taking his eyes off the words before him, not even to comment on his father's appearance. Mrs Crabtree's apron and rubber gloves did very little for Adam's image.

'Thanks. Are you going to dry?'

Matthew waved the suggestion away. 'Later. In a minute. What I mean is, why is it still called Hendrick's "Supernova"? It's an *exploded* supernova, isn't it? A black hole...' His voice died away in puzzlement.

'Right. And we know all about supernovae – how they are formed, what causes them to explode... but black holes, with their immense gravitational forces... they're still pretty much of a mystery.' Adam drifted back into the steamy kitchen. 'We know they are there, from the pull they have on other nearby bodies. But they are invisible. Like some people at washing-up time...'

Matthew looked up. 'You really are worried about Sandra and Margaret, aren't you?'

'What do you mean?'

'I can always tell when you're really concerned. You make feeble jokes...' A wet dishcloth hit Matthew squarely on the ear. Adam stood in the doorway ripping off the gloves and apron, grave-faced.

'They promised to drop in for a nightcap on the way home...' The worry was back, multiplied.

'They'll come.' Matthew pulled Sandra's scarf from his pocket. 'Pity I didn't use something of Margaret's for my psychometric bit. Might have learned more through her than through Sandra.' He realised that he was fighting hard to interest his father, to stop him from plunging out again into the danger of the night.

Adam shrugged, beset by doubts in every direction. 'Learned or imagined...?'

Matthew resented his father's tone. 'I was right about the supernova, wasn't I?' he protested. 'The broken amulet gave me that.'

Adam paced about, not listening much. He opened the corner cupboard and poured himself a Scotch.

'And I was right about the doctor. I saw what happened to him the night he left his gloves behind and the next day he'd changed.' Matthew was not going to let go easily.

'And now the same thing's happened to the girls?'

The boy looked at his father gravely. 'I'm sure it has...'

'But what? What went on after you lost contact?' Adam leaned across the table and punched the buttons of the tape-recorder. The chipmunk noises of the rewind were an accurate rendition of both their thoughts at that moment. Matthew felt the fear return as he heard his own voice, taut and stuttering...

'Such power... white... brilliant... impossible to move... energy... force... sucking... change... changing...'

They stared across the machine at each other, trying to read the meaning in each other's face, seeing only that they were really looking inwardly toward their own minds... the tension that worry can erect around itself.

The voices continued:

'What's the matter? You okay, Matt?'

'It's gone... there's a blank... a dark. I can't get through any more...'

'Try. You've got to keep trying.'

'It's no good... she seems to have stopped feeling...'

'Stopped feeling? What's happened to her?'

'No idea. All I know is... she's gone away. We've lost them.'

Tape hiss was the background to worry and despair for both of them as the meaning of the words sank home.

Behind them the street door swung open and it was the waft of fresh air that made them turn. Framed in the doorway was a smiling Margaret... Adam and Matthew stared at her as though she was a phantom, waiting for the inevitable 'Happy Day' greeting but dreading that their fears would come true.

Margaret's smile faded and a small cloud of concern crossed her face. 'What's this? A seance? Aren't you going to ask me in?'

Adam and Matthew whooped with relief. Matthew punched the tape-recorder OFF button and hurried to pour Margaret a drink, while Adam took her hand and led her to the sofa.

'Am I glad to see you...' he started.

'Correction,' grinned Matthew. 'Are *we* glad to see you... where's Sandra?'

Margaret looked at Adam, puzzled slightly by the question. 'In bed, I imagine.'

'And how was dinner at the big house?'

Margaret waved her hand, dismissing the very idea of dinner. 'Oh, I didn't go. I had a couple of boiled eggs, instead.'

It was the gentlemen's turn to look puzzled. Adam frowned as Matthew chipped in with, 'You didn't go? But...'

They looked at each other. Adam ploughed on. 'You haven't been to Hendrick's house?' Hope welled even in Matthew's mind. He would be quite happy to be proved wrong, if it meant that Margaret and Sandra were unharmed...

'I don't know anybody who has,' said Margaret easily. 'Apart from you. I was looking forward to it, in a strange kind of way.'

Matthew handed her a brandy and took a Scotch across to his father. He studied Margaret covertly. She looked fine. Absolutely normal. Why then did he feel she was lying?

His father was more direct. 'Margaret, you were both invited to dinner. Why didn't you go?'

She sipped appreciatively at her brandy and looked over the rim of the glass at Adam, her gaze steady, savouring the bouquet. 'Sandra really didn't feel too well... I thought an early night would be better for her. So I sent my apologies to Hendrick – but I couldn't pass up your kind offer, could I?' She raised her glass to Adam. 'Cheers!'

Adam did not respond. Dourly on the same track, he said, 'But I don't understand... When you left here, you were on your way to Highfield House.'

'She's been feeling queasy all day. Probably that pop stuff she keeps drinking.' Margaret grinned at Matthew. 'That and the beginnings of a cold.'

It all sounded so possible. Particularly as they wanted so much to believe her.

Adam's face cleared and the tensions melted. Amazed but infinitely pleased, he said, 'So you really didn't go...?'

Matthew felt it was time he left them to play their grown-up games. 'Well,' he said slowly. 'That leaves me with egg on my face...' He nodded at the tape-recorder. 'Sorry, Dad. Goodnight...'

He made his way to the foot of the staircase and stopped, hovering uncertainly. 'Margaret... I'm glad you didn't go. Really.' He stood on one leg, embarrassment growing, wanting to say much more.

Margaret seemed to understand. 'Goodnight, Matt,' she said softly.

When he had gone, she turned back to Adam with only the tiniest glance at the tape-recorder. 'What was that all about? Egg on his face...?'

Adam hesitated a moment, then quickly he hit the REWIND button on the machine. 'Listen,' he said above the nonsense-noise. He stopped the tape and stabbed at the PLAY button, bringing back the immediate past, destroying the present, losing his future forever.

Matthew's voice filled the room: 'Such power... white... brilliant... impossible to move... energy... force... sucking... change... changing...'

The truth sprang out of Margaret's eyes, as they suddenly screwed up in pain and stared into another world. The meaning of the flat, forced words gripped her and she relived some experience beyond his understanding. As she slumped forward, Adam caught her shoulders and managed to kill the description of her agony that the machine was blurting out. He looked down into her suffering face, as he had into his son's. He heard himself say, 'Margaret...' Twice he said it. The loss was in his voice.

Her eyes flicked open and she smiled palely up at him. She took a moment and then managed, 'Don't worry, Adam. I'm all right. I'm perfectly happy...'

Matthew had been right. They were gone...

Mrs Crabtree came as near to thundering as she was able. The morning sun slanted in through the low windows of the cottage and picked out Adam, as he tried to shift a case full of electronic gear to a more advantageous spot among the pile of crates and suitcases.

'Leaving? What do you mean? I never heard the like.'

'I'm afraid so, Mrs C.'

'But you seemed so set here... working so hard, you were. Enjoying yourselves.'

Matthew clattered down the stairs with a travel bag and some oddments for the baggage pile.

The old girl was certainly taking it personally, thought Adam. 'But we'll still need breakfast, Mrs C. How about one of your specials to speed us on our way?'

She turned her full attack on Matthew. 'You'll never be leaving, Master Matthew? Tell your father, he doesn't want to go. You tell him he can't leave Milbury.'

Matthew had never liked Mrs Crabtree and it was difficult to be polite to her. 'I'd like sausages and tomatoes with my eggs and fried bread and some of that chocolate cake if there's any left.'

His father looked surprised at these reasonable breakfast demands. Perhaps his son's eating habits were modifying. 'Sounds good. Twice please. You can have my cake, Matt.'

Mrs Crabtree shook her head and set off for the kitchen. Matthew waited until the door closed behind her.

'My room's packed. Empty. Apart from the one thing that we've forgotten.'

His father licked a label for a crate. 'Which is?' He thumped and smoothed it into place.

'The thing that brought us here, I'm beginning to think...'

Adam waited, pen poised.

'The painting. *"Quod Non Est."* '

'Of course, the painting. It's at the Museum. I took it across to show to Margaret...' Adam's voice tailed away.

Matthew held up Sandra's scarf. 'Tell Mrs Crabtree I'll only be five minutes. I'll return this at the same time.'

The astronomer came out of the darkness of the church and stood for a moment blinking in the bright sunshine. A moment was all that Matthew needed to slip from the churchyard path and behind the shelter of a great yew tree. Hendrick locked the oak door with some difficulty, for the iron key was heavy and awkward to turn, and he was hampered by the two round flat containers that he was carrying. Matthew could see beyond the porch almost to the Museum and realised that he was almost trapped in a situation for which he regarded himself ill-suited. Eavesdropping was not exactly his game; but the situation developed too fast for him to do anything about it, for Sandra appeared out of the Museum, dressed for school. Seeing Hendrick, she ran forward and tried to help him with his burden but he laughed away her efforts and stood joking with her for a moment. Although they were too far away to overhear, Matthew could feel the friendship between them. And when Hendrick bent forward and fondly kissed Sandra on the forehead, it was one of the most surprising and dismaying moments of young Matthew's life.

Sandra waved a cheerful goodbye to Hendrick and sped along the path toward Matthew. He drew even farther back into the shadows as she passed, but he couldn't let her go... Without realizing why, he let out a yell... 'Sandra!'

She stopped and looked back. She obviously could not see him in the shadow of the tree so he stepped out onto the gravel.

'Matthew!' Sandra sounded delighted. She hurtled back along the path and danced around him excitedly. 'Matt! Waiting for me?'

Deliberately, Matthew gave his usual greeting. 'Hi!' He waited, praying inwardly that she would be as she always had

144

been. Sandra just beamed at him. He'd never seen her more pleased with life.

'I... er... this was at our place.' He produced her scarf, a bit bedraggled. 'I thought I'd return it to you and swap it for my painting...'

Sandra was delirious when she saw her scarf. It appeared suddenly to become her most treasured possession. 'Oh... I looked everywhere. Thanks, Matt. You can pick up the painting on the way home from school.'

Hating the lie, Matthew fumbled. 'I'm not going to school. We're... I'm taking the day off to help Dad. Is your mother in? I'll get it now.'

Sandra was already moving away down the path, backwards. 'No, no. She's out. I've got to go, I'll be late.'

Matthew moved a few steps after her. He must ask, despite himself. 'You said the church was locked... not used... What was Mr Hendrick doing in there?'

Sandra shrugged her satchel into a more comfortable position and tossed her hair back. 'Don't know. It's his church. I must rush.'

Matthew stopped. It was useless. Almost to himself he said, 'Sandra... goodbye.'

But she heard. She smiled at him with love and said confidently, gently, 'Not goodbye, Matt. We'll see you soon...'

And then she was off. Matthew watched her until she was out of sight, taking part of his young life with her.

Adam choked on his bacon as Margaret asked, 'Where's Matthew?' from the doorway. Warily, he told her that the boy had gone to her place.

She smiled and held up the painting. 'To get this? I thought he'd forgotten it, so I brought it over.'

Adam stood and took the picture from her. 'Why?'

'Why what?'

'Why did you think he'd forgotten it?'

She held his gaze unwaveringly. 'Well, he hadn't come to fetch it. And I didn't want to miss you… You're leaving today, right?'

Adam challenged. 'Who told you that?'

She smiled. 'You're *not* leaving…?'

He had no answer to that. The silence was leaden.

'Adam, stop playing games. Are you leaving or aren't you?' She sounded genuinely concerned. As though it might make a difference for her.

Adam stared at her blindly, all communication lost. He felt tired. 'Coffee?' he asked politely and without waiting for a reply called to the kitchen, 'Another cup please, Mrs C.'

They both listened to the crockery being taken down and the cupboard door sliding shut in the other room. Mrs Crabtree shuffled and bustled through the door and into their silence.

'Master Matthew, is it?' She stopped dead as she saw Margaret. Then, automatically, she switched on the smiling greeting, 'Well, I never. Welcome, Mrs Smythe… How do you feel this morning?' Adam reacted irritably to the facile secretiveness of the question. Was he not supposed to notice its significance?

'She feels very happy, Mrs Crabtree. But she'd feel even happier with a cup of coffee.'

Mrs Crabtree ignored Adam's chiding tone and poured the coffee for Margaret, never taking her eyes or her smile off her puzzled face. Adam went cold again as he saw Margaret's face clear of its doubt and respond mechanically to the old body's 'happiness.' She was taking her place in the scheme of things…

The church loomed large above Matthew as he searched for a possible entrance. The exterior doors were, of course, locked. The windows, too high to be of any use to an intruder, were not meant to open anyway, but somewhere, he felt sure, there must be a weak spot in the defences.

At the rear of the nave, low down in the wall behind a buttress, he found what he was looking for. Partially obscured by long grass and the overgrowth of ivy was the entrance to the crypt by which coffins were lowered into the vaults. A chute, the only closure an unbolted swing-hinge flap of solid oak…

Matthew looked about him to make certain that he was unobserved, then lowered himself into the mossy stone slipway channel and kicked open the heavy door before him… He slid quickly down and out of sight.

From behind a tombstone dedicated to the memory of a former villager, Sandra's dark head rose, puzzled at the boy's sudden disappearance. She moved slowly toward the point at which he had crouched down by the great stone buttress…

Matthew hit the stone-flagged floor in a heap. Winded, he lay still and listened to the sudden quiet of the crypt. Quiet but not silence, for over all there was the hum of high-voltage electricity and the quiet chatter of machinery in operation.

He raised his head and looked about him. Fixing on the direction of the electronic noises, he pulled himself out of his bruised position and felt his way along the wall, stretching his eyes ahead through the total blackness.

The wall stopped and turned at right angles to the sounds. Matthew cast off into the darkness, hands held in front of him protectively, like a sleepwalker. If he'd closed his eyes he would have seen as much.

His fingers found a great curved stone surface. He felt his way to his right along the wall… suddenly realizing that it was no wall but a huge pillar. The gloom broke and some distance away was not *light*, but a sort of *not-dark*.

Machinery hummed there and he stumbled across the paving toward it. His hands touched a wall and, moments later, metal cable trunking.

The sound came as far as he could make out from a bank of computers and related terminals. Following the trunking forward he discovered that it entered a low tunnel, at the end of which he could make out a dim blue haze.

He hurried along the tunnel, eyes fixed on the low light and blundered into a large-mesh metal screen which brought him up sharply. Beyond the screen was a small vault dimly lit by a low-wattage emergency lamp. In the centre of the stone cavern he could just make out more machinery, heavily boxed in and protected. Cables led to and from it and its working noise was higher-pitched but less obvious than the computer bank.

Beside his head he made out a grille, rather like a ventilation point – but the smell from it was acrid, throat-catching. His eyes started to water and he tried to fight back the need to cough but he could feel his lungs exploding.

The noise echoed in the dark stone spaces like a series of gunshots and Matthew turned to get away from the asphyxiating vent. Stumbling blindly back along the low tunnel, his eyes streaming, he could not see that waiting for him was the great figure of Hendrick.

CHAPTER THIRTEEN

THE LIGHT SNAPPED INTO Matthew's streaming eyes and still he could not see. Hendrick stood at the entrance to the tunnel with his hand on the main switch of a small junction box.

'Good morning, Matthew. How do you like my playroom?'

Matthew froze, wiping his sleeves across his eyes, his heart pounding with the fear of having been caught – not merely trespassing – but spying.

'Now, what are you doing here?' The amused voice became icy.

The boy remembered the advice of an old chess master at his previous school. When about to be mated, *attack*. He tried his best to put on a brave front, realizing that he was probably only making himself look slightly ridiculous. 'Mr Hendrick, I've got to get back, my father's waiting for me.' Feeble, he thought, but the best I can do off-balance.

Hendrick waited. Matthew realised that he was not going to get out of this easily.

'I haven't had breakfast yet.' Now, why on earth had he said that? Feebler than ever. *Attack*, for heaven's sake – but he could think of nothing pithy to say. The boy leaned against the wall for a moment, his legs trembling just like they did in an examination room.

Hendrick was speaking. 'Ah, yes. The estimable Mrs Crabtree… egg, bacon, and tomatoes, no doubt. And chocolate cake?'

He was teasing, surely? Guessing. How else could he know of the breakfast order? Matthew pushed himself away from the wall.

'Don't go just yet. I think you owe me an explanation…'

That was easy. What explanation? He had no explanation. Excuses, yes. But explanation? Matthew gulped in draughts of fresh air; suddenly he felt the need to be out in the sunlight.

The voice hardened. 'Now what were you looking for?'

Matthew hesitated for the last time. Then, *attack*, he thought. Take the bull by the thingummies. 'I was trespassing,' he whispered hoarsely.

Hendrick snapped, 'Patently… but why?'

'I thought this was just a church.' Not entirely true. He could feel himself growing warm and red-faced.

'*Just* a church? Just a place of worship?' Hendrick's voice lost its edge as he thought about this. 'Well, perhaps it is…' He nodded across at the machinery. 'You know what that is, of course?'

Matthew nodded, guardedly.

'A computer. I like to keep in touch… plotting the course of the stars. Predicting positions at any given time. Electronics, magnetism, power… what else has man ever worshipped but power?' His voice was soft, wondering. He sounded as though the boy had touched off a thought in his mind. The question was rhetorical; the last thing he expected was an answer.

It burst out of Matthew. 'Knowledge. Knowledge and truth.'

Hendrick stared at him coldly. 'So that's your excuse. The reason why man continues to pry, to extend the narrow limits of his comprehension, to reach for the stars. But one cannot grasp the ungraspable. There are certain stars that will never be reached.'

He stood for a moment, lost in thought. Then he smiled, changing the mood, and threw an arm around Matthew's shoulders.

'Come. I'll take you back to your father.'

Adam was pouring himself yet another coffee as Matthew walked in, closely followed by Hendrick.

'Don't let me disturb you. Just wanted to see that this young rascal got back to you in time.'

Adam looked quizzically at his son. 'What's he been up to?' The bacon-smell about the place awoke Matthew's passion and he ignored his father's question and went into the kitchen in search of breakfast.

As he went he heard the astronomer say, 'No doubt he'll tell you himself.' He began to relax. If it was up to him to tell his father the truth, that would be no hardship for that was the basis of their relationship and always had been.

The inevitable question came again but was still a surprise to Adam. There was no trace of their hurried departure about the place for Adam had loaded the car with their gear and it stood out of sight around the side of the cottage. So what prompted Hendrick to say, 'So you're going? Leaving us?'

Adam fenced, 'Who told you that?'

'I thought you had a big programme of research?'

'I had.' Two could play the impasse game.

Through his tolerant smile, Hendrick tried, 'You feel you know all you need to know about Milbury?'

Matthew came out of the kitchen fast, juggling the hot plate onto the table. He glanced at his father and could see his tension.

'All I need to know? Yes... perhaps I do.'

Matthew lowered his head into the plate, hating Hendrick. He stabbed a sausage. The fried tomatoes ran like blood.

'So I can't persuade you to remain?'

'I'm afraid not.' His father sounded so defensive. It was awful. Suddenly he could not eat.

The astronomer paced about, seemingly less sure of himself, less patronizing. Suddenly he seemed almost vulnerable. Was this a chink in his armoured exterior? 'I'm truly sorry about that,' he began. He sounded sincere. 'To be honest, I've taken a great liking to you two. I had hoped that once you had settled down here, we could have become… well, closer. People of your ability will be needed here in the future. There's a great deal to be achieved, not only here in the village… but soon… outside the Circle…'

Adam made a gesture of distaste. 'That's what worries me.' Hendrick stopped dead, recognizing the challenge in his voice.

'You're an intelligent man, Brake. Stay and help me in my work. You'll not regret it.'

Matthew watched his father shake his head, positive, dismissive.

'No. We're away.' Adam snapped shut the locks of a briefcase.

Matthew shoved the untouched food away from him. Suddenly he heard himself say, 'What is your work, Mr Hendrick?' His voice surprised him; he had had no intention of butting into his father's discussion.

Adam sounded sharp. 'Matt, stay out of this.'

The astronomer held up a placatory hand. 'No, no. Let him go on… ' The eyes searched into Matthew's brain.

Matthew shrugged. 'What's the use… we all know what I'm talking about. You see yourself as father of the village – no, more than that, you see yourself as the priest here, don't you?' From the flicker in the eyes, Matthew felt that he had touched on the truth…

'What I want to know is, why? Why do you need to be surrounded by a mindless congregation? All on their knees to you, all worshipping whatever it is you stand for, all in a state of…' He groped for the word.

'Happiness…' suggested Hendrick quietly.

Matthew shrugged off the prompt. '*Unknowing*,' he said firmly.

To break the silence, Adam threw the doorkeys on the table in front of Hendrick. Matthew looked at his father, who smiled at him rather sadly… There are moments in a child's growing up which tear at a parent's heart, particularly when lessons are learned the hard way.

Adam suggested, 'Everything's in the car.' Matthew took the cue and grabbed his father's briefcase as he left.

Pulling away from the cottage, Matthew could see Hendrick standing on the doorstep, watching their departure. He certainly looked the part of the patriarch, he had to admit. Even his eyes were smiling...

Adam stopped the car at the junction with the Avenue that snaked through the Circle. He caught Matthew's eye, for this was the spot where he had received the first glimmering of what they had let themselves in for, after the 'now you see it, now you don't' sequence with the lorry.

The car turned right and headed for the entrance to the Circle.

'How did Hendrick know we were going? I didn't tell him, Dad.'

'Maybe he's a psychometrist.' The suggestion was only half-joking.

'Or a magician?'

Adam shook his head, quite serious now. 'Not a magician, no. Magicians deal in magic. Hendrick deals in something far more basic and terrifying... Once we're out of this place, we may be able to rationalise just what it is he's up to... All we've seen so far are the effects.'

'People being made happy.'

'People being drained of all unhappiness... of all disease... of all ambition and thought.' That was certainly nearer the mark.

Frightened, Matthew asked, 'So that there is nothing left for them?'

His father stared grimly ahead. 'No life. Nothing to fight for, no reason to hope, no need to achieve.' He paused as the car sped on. Then added, 'No humanity.'

Matthew could not speak; he was remembering his friends and what had happened to them at Hendrick's hands.

'That's why we are trying to get out of this place...' His father drove on.

Two sarsens flicked past in quick succession and somethng snapped into Matthew's mind. 'This is the way Lyle came,' he said excitedly.

Adam straight-armed the wheel, trying to get the tension out of his shoulders. 'This is where we came in... this is where we met Mrs Crabtree...' He glanced at Matthew's white face. 'This is where we must find the bypass...'

It was then that the nightmare began.

Sarsens flashed by faster and faster. Matthew knew again the pain that became sound, but this time the sound became the vicious scream of the stars in their hurtling chase through the grasp of time. Faces rushed before him, Hendrick's smile, the mouth and teeth... building terror in his mind, tearing agony from his heart... the Solar Serpent... villagers circling... Dai with his amulet crumbling in his hand... the rabbit screaming, writhing in the snare. And all the time the on-rushing to nowhere. The painting fractured into detail that clamoured for his brain... his head burst with faces of the fleeing dreams of old... as the music of the sphere died away into his other-consciousness, leaving a dry slice of sound fluting like a knife through the blackness of his existence...

Then there was the sound, far away, of a car crashing.

Then there was... the relief of silence.

Matthew was the first to stir, and his eyes opened lazily upon complete darkness. But he knew instinctively that he was in a room. He was lying on something soft – a bed? – and not far away, he could hear gentle snores. His questing hand felt the silk of a bedside lamp and the sudden light brought him off the bed into the middle of the room.

His father sat up gingerly on the bed's twin, dishevelled but apparently unhurt.

'Dad, are you all right? Where are we?'

The room was spacious, panelled, furnished with more than comfort in mind.

Adam stared about him, surprised and uncertain. 'We hit a sarsen… a great stone was in the middle of the road…'

Matthew tried to remember, his father was wrong… 'Not a stone. No, it wasn't a stone…'

'We couldn't have missed it. And travelling at that speed…'

Matthew struggled on. 'It was grey, like a stone… but it was human – but not human – it was enormous…' He stood over his father with his arms outstretched, trying to encompass a description of what he thought he had seen.

They both realised at the same moment what it was that Matthew was trying to remember.

'Dad… it was her…'

'Impossible.' Adam shook his head but he knew it was not impossible.

'That's what Lyle saw, too. It was her… but huge, unearthly…'

Adam fought the possibility. 'A delusion.'

Matthew felt the chill creep to the very centre of his being. 'Mrs Crabtree…' he whispered. 'Could it be…?'

The door of the room opened and there stood Hendrick, benign and avuncular. Behind hovered Link with a silver tray set with drinks. All very civilised.

'Good evening,' he beamed. 'My sleeping guests awake…'

Link busied himself with the drink tray while Hendrick moved about the room switching on various lights to make the place less gloomy. It really was a superb room.

'And how are we…? The good Doctor Lyle seemed to think you showed no sign of hurt. I trust he was correct in his assessment?'

Adam cut across the flow of urbanity. 'How did we get here, Hendrick?'

'Fortunately Link here, returning from a shopping expedition, came across your car at the entrance to Linnet

Avenue... You were both unconscious... Fumes, do you imagine? Carbon monoxide from a damaged exhaust?'

Sweetness itself, thought Adam. Most reasonable... but false. 'No, it's simpler than that, I think. We lost our way.'

'Is that possible in Milbury?'

'Not geographically... We missed the turning... the time turning... We failed to get through to our present...'

For a moment, Hendrick looked taken aback, but he quickly recovered, assessing Adam thoughtfully as Link handed around the drinks. 'Dear me. Would you care for Link to contact Dr Lyle? Perhaps he could take another look at you...?'

The inference was obvious. Adam shrugged it aside. 'We seemed to crash. Into... an obstacle. We were doing forty miles an hour when we hit – something – whatever it was. There was no way I could avoid it. Then I blacked out.'

Matthew nodded vehemently. 'That's exactly what happened.'

Hendrick nodded with understanding. 'But your car... totally undamaged. Take a look out of the window, Matthew.'

Despite the gloom outside, there was the car on the gravelled drive, obviously in good order.

'Now, how about telling Lyle about these hallucinations of yours? I feel responsible... you *are* my guests, after all...'

Adam found the unruffled plausibility galling. He burst out, on the verge of losing his temper, 'Keep your doctor, Hendrick. Matthew was close to the truth this morning, wasn't he? Priest is not quite right, though... How do you think of yourself? As Magus?'

The mask slipped for a moment and Matthew could see the ice beneath the suave exterior. Hendrick picked on the hovering Link. 'Get out!' he snapped and the man merged away through the doorway, closing the oak behind him so carefully that Matthew could not hear the handle turn into place.

Hendrick resumed his smile but it was becoming less affable. 'You're going too far, too fast, my dear Brake. There are aspects which even I find difficult to understand... your own arrival in Milbury, for instance.' He seemed genuinely at a loss.

Adam kept up the pressure. Matthew realised that his father had not actually lost his cool but was trying to force Hendrick into emotionalizing the situation. He had spotted the crack in the armour and was now pressing for an opening.

'Get us out of here... that's all we want from you... Magus.'

Adam made it sound like a dirty word but Hendrick was not to be drawn... He was indeed a master...

'Magus, indeed. A scholar-magician leading his people towards beauty and truth...?' He sounded almost sad... lonely... 'You are not halfway right, Professor Brake.' There was a moment while he recovered himself – then the smile again. 'Forgive me, you must want to freshen up.' He pushed open a door which led to the adjoining bathroom and moved to the door through which he had entered. 'I'll leave the tray... I'm sorry you missed our little celebration this afternoon but don't worry. There'll be another tomorrow...' He glanced from his watch to the digital clock on the mantel over the fireplace. 'Dinner in exactly fifty-five minutes.' And closed the door behind him.

Matthew threw himself miserably across the bed. 'So they had a "Happy Day" dance for Margaret and Sandra...?'

Adam nodded grimly and started inspecting the room. 'And tomorrow's will be for us. We've got to get out of here.'

'Dad, there's no way out of the Circle... Dai told me... there's no way out until the stones release us...'

'Mumbo-jumbo. We're in a "now" parallel to our own... a time-shift caused by the energies received here within the Circle... What we must do is hang on to our sanity and use our knowledge... our understanding, to reverse the situation.'

Matthew decided to play the patball game by which they had often thought through a problem together. Bounce the ideas about and sometimes the right spark is struck.

'But how? Escape from the Circle by reversing the effects of this… psychic power?' Not much of a shot, but it was difficult to apply logic to such an illogical situation.

Adam only managed, 'There must be a way…'

'Even if there's no escape from the Circle…?'

'I don't believe that. If there's a way in, there must be a way out.'

Matthew continued hesitantly, 'There's the Sanctuary… It may not be a way out but it's supposed to be a place of safety.'

Adam moved to the window and looked out at the massive circle of stones. 'First we've got to reach it…'

Matthew began to feel the excitement grow. 'It's still inside the stones. There's nothing to stop us.'

Adam's face set grimly as he turned back to his son. 'Nothing? I'm afraid there is, Matt…'

Matthew sprang across the room as, outside, the ancient, ululating chant began. The sound was like a wall, hemming them in. At the window, his father held him in both arms so that the despair would not overpower them both.

In the moonlight, the circle of villagers was forming again…

CHAPTER FOURTEEN

ADAM TURNED AWAY FROM the window, strode across the room, and wrenched the door open. 'Come on.'

Matthew shook his head, the hopelessness of their situation chillingly clear. 'It's no good, Dad.'

'What?'

'We'd never get out.'

'We have to try.'

'Waste of time.'

Adam frowned. 'Matt, what's the matter with you? You're behaving as though you'd been brainwashed already.'

'I'm just facing up to it, that's all.We tried to escape this morning, and what happened? We found ourselves back here. Dai was right: we are trapped… trapped by the stones. We can never leave the Circle till…'

'Till what?'

'Till we've been through… whatever we *have* to go through.'

Adam sat beside him on the bed. 'What do you mean?'

'I don't think there's such a thing as a future in this place,' said Matthew slowly. 'It's all mixed up with the past and the present.'

'Yes, some sort of time-trap. Another continuum.'

'Something like that. The village has two… two *levels*.'

'Two realities, one of which keeps repeating itself.' Adam thought for a moment. 'So if we're right, everything happening now has happened before. It's all predestined.'

'Yes. I've had this strange feeling ever since we arrived. Margaret, Sandra, Mrs Crabtree... Sometimes I knew – I mean, I really knew – what they were going to say next.'

Outside, the chant was gradually increasing in volume. Adam crossed back to the window and looked out. More villagers had joined the circle, and they were looking up at the house in eager anticipation. He started to pace desperately around the room. 'There must be something we can do.'

'I'm sure there is,' said Matthew quietly.

'The question is... what?'

'Dunno. But there has to be a way we can get back to... to the real world. There just *has* to be.'

'Why?'

'Because of the painting. The man and the boy, remember? They were the only ones who looked as if they were escaping.'

Adam stared at him. 'And you reckon that's us?'

'Yes.'

'So all we have to do is find out how they did it?'

'We have to find our own way. Use whatever it is that makes us... special.'

'Our knowledge of astrophysics.'

'Maybe.'

'All right, what have we got to go on? The Circle is aligned to Hendrick's Supernova...'

'... which is now a black hole.' Matthew was suddenly sure this was the key. 'What do we know about black holes, Dad?'

'Not much. They're super-dense collapsed stars whose huge gravitational forces allow nothing – not even light waves – to escape. Anything within their event horizons – their boundaries – is sucked into the centre and crushed out of existence.'

'Imploding energy,' said Matthew, digesting the information. 'Suppose Hendrick's managed to... to *harness* it? Suppose he's using it somehow to turn the villagers into "Happy Day"ers?'

'But why?'

160

'Well, if he's some sort of priest, perhaps he thinks he's doing it for their own good.'

Adam smiled grimly. 'There've been enough men in this century who thought like that.'

'I'm not talking about *this* century, Dad. I'm talking about something that happened thousands of years ago.'

'Hmm. In the beginning was the star…'

'And the star was some sort of God.'

'Ursa XB1!' Adam whirled around excitedly. 'Bear worship. Hendrick *said* it was one of the oldest religions…'

Matthew jumped to his feet, the pieces of the jigsaw beginning to fit. 'Right. Originally, perhaps, it had some sort of benign power. But then, when the supernova became a black hole, the power was reversed…'

'And the priests started using it to extract… well . . *something*. Man's ability to think for himself. The quality that makes him human.'

They stared at each other, awed by the crevasse that was opening up in front of them.

'So *that's* what goes on in Hendrick's peculiar dining room,' said Matthew. 'Whenever XB1 is in alignment with the Circle…'

'And being in the constellation of the Great Bear, that would recur fairly frequently. Daily, probably.'

'He'd still need split-second timing to predict the transit.'

'Which explains the computer in the crypt of the church.'

'And all these digital clocks.'

Adam inspected the clock on the mantelpiece. 'He'd need something more accurate than this.'

'Perhaps there's a master-clock somewhere.'

'Feeding signals all over the house? It's possible.'

'Quartz?'

'Or atomic. Molecules focused by… Wait a minute!'

'What?'

'You said you saw machinery in the crypt. The vent was making your eyes water…'

'Yes.'

'Ammonia. Could that have been what you smelled?'

'And if it was?'

'The atomic clock is sometimes controlled by the ammonia molecule.'

Matthew let out his breath. 'So that's where he keeps it. Dad, if we could alter the…'

But Adam, way ahead of him, was shaking his head. 'Impossible.'

'Why?'

'Atomic clocks can't be altered. Nothing affects the ammonia molecule. That's why they keep super-accurate time.'

Back to square one. Matthew gazed at the digital clock, searching for a way around the problem. 'All these digitals must be driven by a master signal,' he said thoughtfully. 'Can't we interrupt it?'

'Feed in some extra pulses?'

'Yes. So they'll gain time.'

'And so will we. Get Hendrick to… to process us before the black hole's in position up there.'

'Let's find the junction box.'

They searched around the base of the walls.

'Here,' said Adam. 'By the radiator.'

Matthew looked at the wire. 'It feeds down through the central heating system.'

'Good. Now I'll need the oscilloscope. And the oscillator.'

'Wonder what's happened to our luggage.'

'Still in the car. Unless…'

'Unless what?'

'Hendrick's expecting us to stay. Perhaps he had it brought into the house…'

'Well, there's only one way to find out.'

Adam crossed to the door and opened it. He listened for a moment, then peered out into the corridor. 'All clear,' he whispered, and Matthew followed him out of the room.

They tiptoed noiselessly to the head of the stairs and leaned over the banisters. Their luggage was piled up in the hall, just inside the front door. They started to creep down the stairs, but they hadn't gone more than two steps when Adam turned and put his finger to his lips. Matthew froze, listening.

Voices were approaching from the direction of the kitchen. They raced back to take cover behind the balustrade, just as Hendrick and Link appeared below. They held their breath, conscious that the slightest creak would give them away.

'That picture,' Hendrick was saying. 'The one I told you about. It must be here somewhere.'

Link opened Matthew's suitcase, and started rummaging through the contents. 'I'm sure you're worrying unnecessarily, sir. How can an inanimate object harm you?'

'I didn't say it could harm me. But I find it disturbing. It has a hidden meaning, which so far I have been unable to fathom.'

Link found the picture and held it up. 'This?'

'Yes.'

'And what is it that disturbs?'

Hendrick took the picture and propped it up on the mantelpiece, next to the digital clock. 'The man and the boy. I don't understand why they're…'

'Why they're running?'

'Escaping.'

'You think it's a prophecy?'

'I don't know.'

Link smiled. 'There's nothing to fear, sir. Your task is almost complete. What can go wrong now?'

'Yes, you're right.' Hendrick checked his watch with the clock. 'Everything ready in the kitchen?'

'Perhaps you'd care to see for yourself? Set your mind at rest?'

'Very well.'

The two men disappeared back into the recesses of the house, and Matthew breathed a sigh of relief.

Adam stood up, beckoned him to follow, and they ran down the stairs. This time there were no interruptions, and they collected the two aluminum cases without mishap.

'Hope Hendrick doesn't notice they're missing,' said Adam, after they'd reached the relative safety of their room. 'It's lucky he seems so preoccupied with the picture.'

Matthew watched while he detached the wires from the junction box and attached the terminals of the oscilloscope to it. In order to make their calculations, they had to measure the voltage, shape, and frequency of the signal.

'Okay. Switch on.'

Matthew switched on the machine and studied the wave-pattern on the dial.

'What's it look like?'

'200 volts at 55.2 Hertz. And it's a square wave.'

'So it can't be a mains signal.'

'No. Those digitals must be driven by the atomic clock.'

Adam glanced at his watch. 'Hendrick said dinner in fifty-five minutes. Did you notice from when?'

'There's about half an hour left.'

'Got a pencil?' Matthew produced a pencil-stub from his pocket. 'Now... I want an extra five minutes. Work out what frequency we need.'

He started to unpack the oscillator, while Matthew did some rapid calculations on the wall above the junction box.

'Dad...'

'Don't talk. This is one sum you have to get right.'

'But it's interesting. Early man worshipped the Great Bear, right?'

'Right.'

'Did you know that the Gaelic word for bear is Math? I looked it up. Get it... Maths?'

'Got it,' said Adam. 'The question is... have you?'

Matthew checked the figures carefully. 'We need a 64.1 Hertz signal. That'll give us just over five minutes.'

'Let's hope it's enough.' Adam hit a switch, and the oscillator began to emit a low-pitched hum. 'And let's hope Hendrick's not clock-watching.'

The numbers on the digital clock began to flick past at an appreciably faster rate. Matthew watched them for a moment, then wandered over to the window.

Outside, the circle was almost complete. Two stragglers emerged from the shadowy undergrowth at the edge of the garden and took their places in the ring. The light from the house that spilled over the lawn illuminated the vacantly blissful expressions on their faces. Matthew stiffened as he recognised them.

'Dad. Look.'

Adam joined him, and stared down grimly at the two figures below. They were Margaret and Sandra.

'So now they're Happy Ones,' he murmured softly, 'waiting for the last of the minnows to be devoured.'

Matthew thought sadly of the first time he had seen Sandra, peering over his shoulder at the painting, and of his first meeting with Margaret, ministering to his father after he had touched the stone. He remembered the times they had all puzzled over the mystery together, and realised how close they had been to solving it. Close, but not close enough. And now it was too late.

Images that he had seen through Sandra's scarf flashed through his mind; and he could feel again the sudden, heart-stopping fear that had been transmitted from the dining room. He saw her figure being irradiated by the white, dazzling beam... and instinctively, he knew what had happened to her.

'Of course!' he said, turning to Adam. 'It's the other way up.'

'What is?'

Matthew tried to marshall his thoughts. 'The black hole. Gravity so great that not even light particles can escape. So the dish under the village isn't a receiver. It's a transmitter.'

'Transmitting what?'

'Evil.'

Adam absorbed this in silence for a moment. 'Or Hendrick's idea of evil. The capacity to do wrong.'

'Yeah. He uses the inverted gravitational force of XB1 to... to drain it away.'

'The priest's sacrifice to his God. But hold on a minute... Where's the power source? Where does he get the power for the transmission?'

'The leylines. They bring the power – psychic power – into the Circle.'

Adam stared at him. 'A pagan storehouse of energy. And to think I laughed at the idea...'

He spun around in alarm as footsteps echoed down the corridor. 'Quick! Get that stuff out of sight.'

Frantically, they detached the wires from the junction box and stowed the equipment under the beds. They were just in time, for a moment later Hendrick entered, smiling affably.

'Dinner is served. Will you follow me, please?'

Obediently, they followed him along the corridor, and up the great staircase to the top floor. There, Link was waiting to usher them into the dining room. Hendrick stood aside, and motioned Adam and Matthew to precede him.

Matthew stared around the room. Although he had seen it before in his vision, he was amazed to discover how accurate his precognition had been. There was the round stone table, the high-backed throne, the sliding panel in the ceiling... It was hard to believe he had never set foot inside it until now.

'Aren't you going to say 'What an extraordinary room?' ' asked Hendrick. 'Most people do.'

Adam's face was expressionless. 'In what way extraordinary?'

'Well, take my throne. An unusual piece, don't you think?'

'Splendid. But it's exactly the sort of thing I should have expected a man with your conceit to have chosen.'

Matthew glanced at his father. He knew exactly what he was trying to do: goad Hendrick, take the offensive, keep him off balance. It was the right strategy.

'You think I'm conceited?' Hendrick sounded as if it were a matter of supreme indifference to him.

'I think you have an exaggerated sense of your own importance. I mean, you're so predictable. Even Matt can tell what your next move will be.'

'Really?' Hendrick surveyed Matthew coolly.

Matthew felt it was time he did his party piece. 'You'll sit on your throne between Dad and me,' he said, 'and explain that the table acts as a transmitter, focusing the psychic energy gathered by the stone dish under the Circle.'

Hendrick didn't look at all put out. 'Well, let's see if you're right, shall we?' He motioned them to the table. 'Bon appetit, my children.'

They took their places on either side of the throne, and Link served them with some steaming hot broth. When he had finished, Matthew saw him raise his eyebrows questioningly at his master. Hendrick glanced at the digital clock, nodded, and Link discreetly withdrew.

Matthew sipped his broth in silence, listening apprehensively as the sound of chanting wafted up from below.

'Another village ceremony?' asked Adam calmly. 'Don't you think you're overdoing them?'

'There are many just now,' said Hendrick, his eyes fastened on the clock. 'The summer solstice, you know.'

'The time of ancient magic?'

Hendrick shrugged. 'The rituals are important. Tradition is very strong in this part of the country.'

'You still practise human sacrifice?'

'Crude and unnecessary. Our methods are much more civilised.'

'Methods of what?'

'Purging the community of sin.'

'The task of priests.'

'Indeed. It is our duty to accept the burden and take it on our own shoulders.'

Adam paused, his spoon halfway to his mouth.

'*Our*?' But Hendrick was no longer listening. He suddenly bowed his head, and began to speak in a low, rumbling voice that sounded like a distant avalanche.

'Anger of Fire... Fire of Speech... Breath of Knowledge... Render us free from harm. Return to us the innocence that once we knew. Complete the Circle. Make us at one with nature and the elements...' Then, looking up... 'It is time.'

The strange procedure that Matthew had been able to see through Sandra's scarf began again. The panel in the ceiling rolled back, to reveal a section of the night sky immediately above the table. At the same time, Hendrick's throne revolved, so that its high back formed a protective shield between him and his guests. The chanting of the villagers below was reaching a crescendo.

Matthew looked at Adam in alarm. But his father put his finger to his lips and tapped his watch reassuringly. If he had done his homework properly, they had five minutes' grace before Ursa XB1 was due to appear on the alignment path.

The chanting suddenly stopped and there was complete silence for what seemed like an eternity. Adam signalled to Matthew to remain calm, but it required a supreme effort of will to remain in his seat. Any moment now, XB1 would appear...

At last, Hendrick's throne started to revolve again. Matthew quickly slumped across the table, and Adam followed suit. They heard the throne click back into position, and Hendrick's voice, soft and deep: 'Arise, my children.'

Slowly, they raised their heads from the table. 'I commune and identify with the forces of nature,' continued Hendrick, looking up through the open panel at the night sky. 'Your sin is my sin. Your guilt is my guilt. You are free. I have fulfilled my function.'

He turned to Matthew, who managed a beatific smile, despite the fact that he felt achingly vulnerable. He kept the smile in place while a dreadful thought occurred to him: suppose he'd made a mistake in his calculations?

'You are happy?' asked Hendrick quietly.

Matthew nodded. 'Happy. Very happy…'

'Very happy,' repeated Adam.

Hendrick smiled, and there was both triumph and relief in his face. 'Happy Day indeed. My flock is cleansed. My task is done…'

He pressed a button on the arm of his throne, and almost immediately Link appeared. 'Take them outside.' Adam and Matthew stood up, grateful for the chance of moving out of XB1's range.

'When you join the circle,' said Hendrick as they joined Link at the door, 'your initiation will be complete. You will be Happy Ones…'

As they followed Link out of the room, Matthew glanced back, and saw that Hendrick had collapsed across the table. He looked drained and exhausted…

Outside, the villagers were waiting for them, silent and motionless, their hands still joined in a circle. Margaret and Sandra broke the chain, and held out their arms in a gesture of welcome. Matthew hesitated, but he felt Adam's hand in his back, propelling him on. With Link watching, they had no alternative but to complete the ceremonial process.

But as soon as they joined the circle, Matthew sensed dismay and consternation among the villagers. Sandra stared at him, looking puzzled and disturbed, and let go of his hand. Then one by one, the other villagers released their neighbours' hands and stood about uncertainly.

'We've broken the circuit,' Adam whispered. 'They're wondering where the power's gone.'

Matthew turned, to find Link regarding them like a computer discarding possible alternatives. Then, seeming to select the right punch-card, he turned and ran into the house.

'He's on to us,' said Adam, looking at his watch. 'But I reckon he's just too late…'

Link rushed into the hall just as the grandfather clock started whirring in preparation for striking the quarter hour. He glanced at the digital clock on the mantelpiece, and saw that it differed in time by nearly five minutes.

He cursed softly. So his master had been right: these last two *were* a threat. But how had they done it! His eyes fell on the luggage by the door. Of course: the two missing cases. He should have been more careful, taken Hendrick's warnings more seriously.

He ran up the great staircase to the dining room. Hendrick was still slumped across the table, but raised his head in alarm as Link burst in.

'Master. They are still impure…'

'*What?*'

'The circle is broken. Your protection is gone. You must leave immediately…'

Hendrick stood up, aghast as he realised the danger he was in, but he was too late. He was still in contact with the table as XB1's dazzling beam flashed through the open panel in the ceiling and irradiated his massive figure. The table cracked asunder, and he let out a wild howl of agony, pain, and despair.

Link watched, transfixed with horror, as his silhouette dissolved into those of his priest-predecessors: medieval, Saxon, and finally the robed shape of a Stone Age spiritual leader. Then, this too dissolved, leaving only the blinding brilliance in the centre of the room. The primitive howl began to fade, echoing down the centuries, until there was silence. The silence of eternity…

CHAPTER FIFTEEN

OUTSIDE, THE VILLAGERS WERE staring up at the house, transfixed by the pillar of light that poured down into the top room, and by the dying animal cries that came from it. As Adam and Matthew watched, the light began to pulse, and with each pulse it grew stronger, until the whole house began to glow in the darkness, suffused with a shimmering aura of irradiated energy.

A confused murmur came from the villagers, and they started to back away in panic. Margaret and Sandra remained where they were, staring at the house as if hypnotised. Adam turned, grabbed Margaret's arm, and started to pull her away.

'Come on! Matt, you take Sandra...'

Matthew took Sandra's hand and dragged her off into the darkness. Her head remained turned toward the house, as if she were unable to take her eyes from it, and he tried to swing her around.

'Don't look back. Sandra... whatever you do... *don't look back*!'

They stumbled on, surrounded by the fleeing villagers. The night was filled with shrieks of terror and alarm, but Matthew ploughed through the undergrowth with grim determination, pulling the reluctant Sandra after him. The task became more and more difficult as her resistance increased, and he turned to try to urge her out of her trance-like state.

To his horror, he saw that she was glancing back.

'No! Sandra, don't!'

But he was too late. The hand he was holding seemed to grow larger, so that he was forced to let her go. Her whole body began to increase in size and shape, and she started to scream…

A few yards away, Margaret heard the scream and turned to look. As she saw what was happening to her daughter, she cried out in despair: 'Sandra!' Adam tried to drag her away, but a greater force had rooted her to the spot. He, too, was forced to let go, as her silhouette grew and began to petrify.

His face averted from the light, Adam held out his arm behind him. 'Matt! Hold on to me!'

Matthew, who had also been careful not to look back, took his hand.

'We can't just leave them, dad…'

'There's nothing we can do. The Sanctuary. Which way?'

Matthew pointed, and immediately felt himself jerked off his feet as Adam lurched forward into the darkness. The grip on his hand grew tighter and tighter, as they pounded on and on together, stumbling, falling, panting for breath, until the agonised cries behind them became faint, barely audible echoes.

They passed the place where they had seen Dai's body, and Matthew noticed that even the low boulder had disappeared. But there was no time to stop – no time to make sense of anything. If they didn't reach the Sanctuary, they were lost.

At last, the entrance to Linnet Barrow loomed in front of them. They staggered in and collapsed onto the floor, utterly exhausted. Matthew lay where he fell, feeling as if he had been drugged, as if his brain was running down. His memory had been shattered into a thousand terrifying fragments, and he found he couldn't piece them together. All he could remember was the picture. *His* picture. It seemed to fill his mind, weighing on his eyelids and forcing them to close. They were safe: that was all he knew. So there was no point in trying to stay awake any more. No point in reliving a nightmare. Perhaps in the morning he'd find it hadn't happened.

But when he awoke, he found himself in the middle of another nightmare. Or rather daymare, for sunlight was streaming in through the barrow entrance. The fact that the darkness had gone, however, did nothing to lessen his fear when he discovered that someone was holding a knife at his throat.

He remained motionless on the ground, holding his breath and not even daring to move his eyes.

'What do you think you're up to, boy?' asked a familiar voice.

Matthew ventured a glance sideways, and gasped with relief. 'Dai! It's you! You're alive…'

'Alive? 'Course I'm alive. Thought I was dead, did you? Thought I wouldn't need my home any more?'

Matthew struggled up into a sitting position. Dai was crouched beside him, holding a motley collection of wicked-looking knives. Or was it Dai? There was something… different about him. Gone was the filthy raincoat, its place taken by an equally filthy seaman's jacket. And the harsh Welsh lilt was absent: this man spoke with a bad-tempered whine.

Yet the face was the same and the suspicious expression an exact replica of the one that had greeted him when he crawled out of the hedge after being knocked off his bike. Perhaps this was another test, to see if he could be trusted. He decided to give the answer which had seemed to satisfy the old man when they first met.

'You nutter! What did you want to give me a fright like that for?'

But this time, Dai seemed far from satisfied. He continued to hold the knife pointed at Matthew's chest. 'I asked you a question, boy. What do you think you're doing here?'

'We came because… because it was safe.'

'Safe? What is this? Some kind of riddle?'

'You know it is. And you gave us the answer.'

'No time for riddles,' said Dai crossly. 'Got work to do. All those knives, see? Got to get them sharp.'

For the first time, Matthew noticed that the Sanctuary, too, looked different. There were no rabbits or pheasants – even the hooks seemed to have disappeared – and a strange-looking contraption stood in a corner.

'What's that?' he asked.

'That? My grinder, of course. Seen it often enough before.'

'Where did you get it?'

'Belonged to my father, that did. And his father before him…'

Matthew frowned. 'But what's happened to all the rabbits and pheasants?'

'Rabbits and pheasants? You all right, boy?' Dai peered at him, wary and hostile.

'You *are* Dai?' Matthew was becoming more and more confused.

'Pretending you don't know me now, is it? Off you go, and take your father with you.' He moved aside, and Matthew saw that Adam was asleep on the ground a few feet away. He scrambled to his feet and shook him awake.

'Dad.' Adam sat up with a start, and stared around the barrow bewildered. 'It's Dai.'

'Dai?'

'You met before, remember? He came to the cottage the day after you found me with the bandage around my head.'

'Get back home, Professor,' said Dai belligerently, 'and leave me to my work.'

Matthew wandered over to inspect the knife-grinding machine. 'You know who we are then?'

'I know who you are, all right. People with no knives to sharpen. I could starve, for all you care.'

Adam stood up. 'You never asked us.'

'Asked you what?'

'Whether we had any knives for you.'

Dai moved to stand in front of him, and poked him in the chest with the point of his knife. 'Better go, Professor. Before I lose my temper.'

Adam turned to Matthew. 'Come on, Matt,' he said, and led the way out of the barrow.

They stood in the entrance, blinking in the bright sunlight. The village basked serenely in the summer air, and the countryside looked quiet and peaceful.

'It's changed,' said Matthew softly.

'What?'

'The village. It's not the same.'

'How do you know?'

'I can feel it. The... innocence.'

Adam glanced at him. 'Well, let's see if you're right, shall we?'

Then, as they set off down the Avenue... 'Where first?'

'The Museum.'

'Thought you might say that.'

'Well? Isn't that where you want to go?'

'Could be.'

But when they arrived at the Museum, they found not Margaret and Sandra... but Mrs Crabtree, sitting at the desk. Adam and Matthew stared at her, fearing the worst. But she stood up in excitement when she saw them, and there was no 'Happy Day' nonsense.

'Why, Professor! Master Matthew! Where have you been? We've been so worried.'

And she really did look worried – even human. To Matthew, it seemed as if the brainwashing process had been washed off. That is, if it was the same woman. But if it wasn't, how could she have been so worried about them? And if it was, why did he no longer feel any hostility toward her? This twinkling, friendly person bore no relation to the dead fish who had looked after them for the past weeks.

Mrs Crabtree opened the door marked 'Private' at the back of the Museum, and called upstairs. 'Mrs Smythe! You can cancel that call. They're back safe and sound.'

There was a loud yelp of delight, and the sound of someone clattering downstairs.

Mrs Crabtree turned to Adam. 'Your car was still there this morning, outside the cottage. Luggage and all. We couldn't think where you'd got to. Worried to death, we were…'

Margaret appeared at the bottom of the stairs, rushed into Adam's arms, and hugged him as if she never wanted to let go of him again. 'Oh Adam,' she said, burying her head in his anorak. Then, looking anxiously up at him: 'What happened?'

Adam managed a faint smile. 'It's a long story.'

'Tell me.'

'You wouldn't believe it.'

Or would she? Was this the attractive creature who had welcomed him so warmly when he first came to the village, or the terrified victim he had tried to save from her preordained fate? No, the 'happy' Margaret had disappeared, and the vacant stare that had clouded those beautiful green eyes had gone. There was nothing there now but a troubled innocence – an innocence reborn.

And yet, at the same moment Adam recognised the woman he had come to love, he realised with exquisite agony that he could never claim her. Her destiny lay here, inside the Circle; his outside, in another world. He could see her – even touch her – but Time had flung them into separate compartments and built a sheet of unbreakable glass between them. There was nothing either of them could do about it.

She seemed to share his pain, but not his awareness. 'Why wouldn't I believe it?' she asked softly.

'Because you belong here. And I don't.'

'So you're destined to leave us?' There was infinite sadness in her voice. A deep sense of loss.

'If we can.'

She didn't understand, but tried bravely to hide her misery. 'I'm glad we had such a hold on you.'

'Yes. You'll never know how near we were to staying.'

'Well,' she said, offering her hand. 'It's been nice.'

'For me too.' Adam covered her hand with his, and kept hold of it so long that she had to make a conscious effort to break away. She turned to Matthew.

'Goodbye, Matt.'

'Bye,' he said, uncomfortably aware of the inadequacy of his reply. He'd never been good at farewells, and this one was particularly awkward. He, too, knew they'd never see each other again.

'Sandra'll be furious she missed you,' Margaret went on. 'She wanted to thank you for helping her with her homework.'

'Really?'

'Yes. I don't know how she'll manage without you. According to her, you're the best in the class.'

Matthew glanced at Adam in relief. So things *were* back to normal.

Adam grinned. 'The others must be very backward.' He gave her hand a final squeeze and jerked his thumb at Matthew, who followed him out into the street.

Neither of them said a word on the way back to the cottage. Matthew, realizing what a wrench the parting had been for his father, left him alone with his thoughts. This wasn't easy, as it meant keeping his growing apprehension to himself. Suppose their car wasn't there? Suppose it wouldn't start? Suppose, when they reached the edge of the Circle, the same thing happened again?

But the car *was* there. And it *did* start. Two fears that proved to be unfounded. But what about the third…?

As they passed Highfield House, Matthew saw that there was an Estate Agent's 'For Sale' board standing by the gate.

'Dad! Look!'

Adam brought the car skidding to a halt, and frowned at the board. 'Take a look?'

Matthew shrugged. It would postpone the dreaded moment when they had to pass through the Circle. 'Okay.'

They got out of the car and walked up the drive. The front door was slightly ajar, and Adam pushed it open with his foot, as if he expected Hendrick to jump out from behind it.

The hall was dusty and bare. All the furniture had disappeared, and it looked as if no one had lived there for years. Cautiously, they entered and started wandering around, their footsteps echoing on the floorboards. It was hard to believe that only yesterday... or was it yesterday? Perhaps it was thousands of years ago. Perhaps it was tomorrow.

Matthew noticed a picture lying face down on the floor near the mantelpiece. *His* picture. He rushed over and picked it up.

But it wasn't his picture. It was a painting of the village all right, but a dull, modern reproduction of picture-postcard quality. Nothing primitive or nightmarish about it.

Adam peered over his shoulder. 'You thought it might be yours?'

'Well, that's where we last saw it. And the frame's the same.'

'Coincidence?'

'You don't really believe that?'

'I don't know what I believe any more.'

'Sir Joshua Lytton?' said a voice from somewhere above them.

They whirled around in alarm, to see a man standing at the head of the great staircase. His face was hidden in shadow, and all they could make out was the tall, lean figure dressed in a light-grey overcoat.

'I beg your pardon?' Adam moved toward the foot of the stairs.

As the man moved down toward him, revealing his face, Matthew gasped. It was Link. Or someone like Link. Less suave. A moustache. And a slight country burr in his voice.

'Sir Joshua Lytton?'

'Adam Brake.'

The man stopped and stared at him. 'Mr Hardcastle sent you?'

'Wrong again, I'm afraid. Who's Mr Hardcastle?'

'The estate solicitor. My name's Link…'

Matthew's heart jumped, but Adam remained calm. 'Ah, ' he said, as if he'd never heard the name before.

'Manager of the estate. You're not a prospective purchaser?'

'No. We – er – used to know the previous owner. Thought we'd drop in for old time's sake. But if we're trespassing…?'

'Please.' Link waved his arm expansively. 'Look around, if you want to. I'm expecting a client at any moment.'

'Sir Joshua?'

'You know him too?'

'He's not by any chance an astronomer?'

'Astronomer? What ever gave you that idea? No, he's an eminent psychiatrist. I understand he intends to retire shortly.'

'I see.'

'Between you and me, I think this is just the sort of place he's looking for.'

Adam looked around the oak-panelled walls. 'Yes. It's certainly a beautiful house.'

'And full of memories for you, I expect?'

Matthew gazed at him, wondering whether any double meaning was intended. But the polite smile seemed to contain nothing but casual interest.

'Memories,' Adam was saying. 'Yes, it's full of those.' He moved to the door. 'Well, thank you and… goodbye.'

'Goodbye.'

Just for a moment, Matthew thought he detected a gleam of animosity in the man's voice. But no; he must have imagined it. This practical man of the world had nothing in common with the sinister butler except his name. He turned and hurried out.

Back in the car, Adam gave Matthew's knee a reassuring pat. 'Well, here goes.'

'Just… take it easy, Dad,' said Matthew nervously.

'Right. Slow but sure.'

They drove at ten miles an hour out to the edge of the Circle. A hundred yards from the point where the road passed through the stones, Adam slowed down even more, and they crawled slowly toward the open countryside. Matthew swallowed and shut his eyes, unable to look. He started counting to himself, calculating that by the time he reached fifty they would either be safe, or… or they would know they were trapped forever.

But he had only got to thirty-six when Adam nudged him. 'All right. You can look now.'

Matthew opened his eyes, and sighed with heartfelt relief. The Circle was behind them and they were driving down the main road, gathering speed. They had made it!

At the top of the hill, Adam stopped the car and they looked back at the village, lying sleepily inside the stones. Was that really the Milbury they had visited? Was that their cottage… that the schoolroom… and that the Museum? And which was harder to believe – that the nightmare *had* taken place there? Or that it *hadn't*?

'Did it happen, dad?' asked Matthew softly, 'or didn't it?'

Adam shook his head. 'I don't know, Matt. I just don't know.'

'Perhaps there was another circle. Besides the stones.'

'What?'

'Time. Perhaps that was circular too.'

'You mean, it may happen again some day?'

'It may already be happening,' said Matthew thoughtfully. 'To the people inside the time-trap.'

Adam grinned. 'You want to go back and see?'

'What *I* want is a sandwich.'

'Don't tell me! Peanut butter… strawberry mousse… pickled cucumbers… golden syrup…'

He let out the handbrake, and the car rattled off down the other side of the hill.

EPILOGUE

AS THE DAIMLER NEARED the crossroads, another, grander car passed it travelling in the opposite direction. It moved sedately down the Avenue, passed through the Circle, and drew up outside Highfield House. A big, distinguished-looking man got out and rang the bell.

The door opened immediately. 'Mr Link?' enquired the stranger. 'Sir Joshua Lytton…'

'Ah, good morning, sir. Come in, won't you?'

Link stood aside, to allow the visitor to enter. He watched expressionlessly, as the big man wandered around the hall, inspecting the place with approval.

'Pleasant drive?'

'Delightful. Can't tell you what a relief it is to get out of London. Modern life is such an appalling rat race.'

'Well, you couldn't retire to a nicer part of the world.'

'No, indeed.' The stranger turned, his mind made up. 'It's ideal. I believe I shall be very happy here.'

And they smiled at each other.

Also available from

fantom
publishing

Return
to the
Stones

by Jeremy Burnham

The long-awaited sequel to *Children of the Stones*, now published in book form for the first time.

Thirty years after his experiences inside the Milbury Stone Circle as a teenager, Matthew Brake is now an astrophysicist like his father Adam before him – and a father himself. Recently divorced, Matthew brings his young American son Tom back to Milbury, where Adam now lives – and a new enemy awaits.

ISBN 978-1-78196-136-0

Available in paperback from
www.fantomfilms.co.uk

Also available from

fantom
publishing

Raven

by Jeremy Burnham and Trevor Ray

THE ORIGINAL NOVEL INSPIRED BY THE TELEVISION CLASSIC

The ancient underground caves are in danger, with plans afoot
to use them for the disposal of atomic waste. But forces are at
work to save the sacred ground – forces from another time.

Why do the caves contain mysterious symbols and how
does the legend of King Arthur connect with them? What
power does Professor Young, the archaeologist, have to save
the cave complex? And why does the merlin suddenly appear?

Raven, on probation from Borstal, finds himself caught up
with these strange powers, and begins to realise that the future
of the caves depends on him…

ISBN 978-1-78196-114-8

Available in hardback from
www.fantomfilms.co.uk